In Pursuit Of
Friendship

Nantes Quinot Jnr.

BookTree
Publishing

PO Box 105
Narangba Qld 4504
Australia

www.booktreepublishing.com.au

ACKNOWLEDGEMENTS

To the people who have helped make this project a reality.

Ioline, my wife, with her unending patience.

Cornelis, my son with his knowledge of the computer systems, and the constant calls for help, that he answered.

To Katy, of Book Tree Publishing, for her help and guidance through the process of design with it's myriad of potential options, as well as the printing of this book.

I am deeply indebted and say thank, for believing in me.

ONE

In the big city, life was a rat race and Tom Edwards did not appreciate it. His family consisted of his dad, his mum, and an older sister. His dad and mum were good, hard-working people and his home life was one of love, compassion and tolerance. There was no drama. Since they lived near the beaches, on the north shore, it was only right that his dad taught Tom to surf and participate in the surf life saving programme. Father and son would go surfing in the week after work if it was still light. Surfing was one of Tom's passions and he knew that wherever he decided to live it would need to be near the sea. Mr. Edwards saw Tom showed promise at school so he spoke to him about what future he saw for himself. As a toolmaker, Mr. Edwards had earned the praise of his peers for his prowess at his trade and Tom knew that his dad was very skilled at what he did. However Tom would wait a while before making a decision as to his future. He liked to work with his hands but he wished to do so to an end. Tom's dad taught him many things in their little workshop at home and they were good mates not just father and son. So as time went by, Tom decided he would like to pursue a course in electrical engineering, but he wanted to start on the tools and work his way up, to become an electrical engineer. His dad encouraged him and Tom began a programme for aspiring young engineers. Tom was no idiot, and he progressed very well in his chosen field. After five years Tom qualified as a talented, Electrical Engineer. On completion of his degree Tom decided he had no desire to live in the big city and wanted to move north. His dad said he should follow his dreams and seek a place that suited him. So Tom moved north, until he found beautiful Emerald.

Five years on, Tom arrived home earlier one afternoon and was thinking of having a swim before Shirley, Tom's wife, arrived home. She would be doing stocktake for about an hour, after work with her dad. He parked in the driveway and as he alighted from the car, he heard some loud noises coming from next door, where the elderly Hughes couple lived. This did not sound right as this was usually the afternoon the couple played carpet bowls at the club. They did not arrive home till after six. The Hughes couple were about 75 years old and lived quietly, going out, to do grocery shopping and to the club to play carpet bowls. Tom had been nearby the day David Hughes had fallen while mowing, in the front garden. He had taken David to the Emergency Hub Services Centre in Emerald for a check up. David was given a clean bill of health and his wife, Helen was very relieved.

The couple were pleasant people and Tom made a habit of checking on them a few times a week to ensure all was well. Tom walked around the side of the house to the backyard and there were two young kids trying to break in. Before they realised it, Tom was on top of them and grabbed them each by the scruff of the neck. Tom did not recognise them, and they were no more than 10 or 12 years of age. So he loaded them in the back of his car and took them down to the police station. Sgt. Lewis was just coming out of the station as he arrived and asked "what are you up to Tom". "These kids need a serious talking to" Tom explained, saying he caught them trying to break in next door, at the Hughes residence.

Just then Gerry arrived at the police station and Sgt. Lewis introduced Gerry Keane to Tom Edwards.

He explained to Tom. "This was a most opportune moment, as Gerry was a local businessman, who was involved in a programme counselling youngsters. Who were in trouble for minor infractions of the law." Sergeant Lewis said he would go and deal with the two boys and Gerry would be contacted, to provide them with counselling. So Tom invited Gerry around to his home for a beer and a chat. Tom produced the beer and they took a seat on the verandah.

The first question from Tom was"how did you get involved in a programme counselling youth"? Gerry answered "he had an interest in criminology, and had done a degree by way of correspondence in psychology and criminology. Subsequently he had approached the local police station offering to help with young offenders. As he was not in the police force, there was a chance they would listen to him more easily. The police were impressed with the initial results, so they asked Gerry to continue the programme, and they would reassess the situation in six months time." This idea proved effective, and now he regularly spoke to young offenders, with encouraging results. But Gerry was not happy, "he said they needed to give the youth something to occupy their time, and possibly give them a goal, or something to live for. If they just stopped the youth from break and enters, then that would leave a vacuum, in their lives." "Maybe introducing them to lifesaving, could be beneficial"Tom said. Gerry liked this idea and said "it has good merit. This would cultivate a sense of belonging, and responsibility to the community, as well as develop self control." Both Tom and Gerry agreed the idea of getting the wayward youth into lifesaving, could be a winner so Gerry said he would mention this to Sergeant Lewis.

By the time Shirley arrived home from work, Tom and Gerry were sitting there like two old school buddies discussing everything under the sun. Tom introduced Shirley to Gerry, and she joined them on the verandah. Tom explained who Gerry was and how they came to meet. Gerry told them Beverley, who was his wife, ran a boutique in north Emerald. Their daughter, Jane who was showing great potential on the violin, was a student at the primary school in Emerald. Shirley said she knew of the boutique and had been in there a few times. Gerry invited Tom and Shirley around to his home, on the coming Saturday afternoon to meet Bev and Jane, Tom and Shirley gladly accepted, and Gerry left. Tom went back to the neighbours, to tell them about the two youths he had caught, at their back door trying to force entry. David Hughes was very grateful for Tom's intrusion. On inspection, they found little damage had been done, and David said he would give the area a coat of paint to make it look good again. Tom mentioned that he had taken the two offenders down to the police station, for a stern rebuke. The Hughes' were a little bit upset by this event, but were grateful for Tom's intervention and the outcome.

The following Saturday proved to be a wonderful success, as they all got on so well together, then Gerry and Bev asked them to stay on for a barbecue, and they gladly accepted. As they were sitting around the barbecue talking. Tom told, how he had lived in the big city. Where he did his degree by way of practical experience and lectures after hours at university. His parents had passed away a few years back and he had a sister in the United States, married to a chemical engineer. He disliked the big city, and came up the coast looking for a town, not too small, where the surfing was good. Emerald seemed the ideal spot, with it's huge lake and many beaches, so he decided to stay. As it had plenty in its favour, he would make a life here, at a pace that was more comfortable. Since that day he had, built a security business, from scratch, catering for commercial, industrial and domestic situations. Furthermore, and more importantly, he had married Shirley and that was the best thing he had ever done.

Gerry's upbringing differed from Tom's, as his father was a surgeon at the Arncliffe Hospital. He and his sister were very well looked after and Gerry's father hoped Gerry would one day become a surgeon. Early on his parents noticed he was a gifted boy, so there was no reason why he could not achieve this distinction. However, Gerry had no desire to be a surgeon. He was more inclined to accountancy or possibly psychology. In the end Gerry registered for accountancy, which he completed, very comfortably. However once they moved to Emerald, he told Bev he felt he needed to do a degree in psychology and criminology, so he completed the degree with honours. His interest in these subjects gave Gerry much food for thought, and that is how he got involved with the programme counselling disadvantaged youth.

Gerry said " he, and Bev had come from Arncliffe, 100 kilometres down towards the big city, where they had grown up and attended University. Shortly after qualifying his dad passed away, and his mum moved to live with his sister in the big city. Gerry's father had left him well off, and as there was nothing keeping them in Arncliffe, they decided to come to Emerald, a small town with plenty of potential where they could establish themselves. They had now been in Emerald for a number of years and felt comfortable here."

This friendship of the two families would have to endure very difficult times, none of them of their own making. They all enjoyed being out on Tom's boat or having a barbecue at one of their homes. Tom was mechanically minded and Gerry was more academically gifted so they were opposites, maybe this was why they got on so well together. Gerry would help Tom with advice about investing in property or business, as he had a natural gift for this and he was able to point out any possible pitfalls, Tom would be happy to advise Gerry about anything mechanical or electrical, be it an engine noise in the car or about solar power. The two of them could always be found in some discussion, until forced to disengage. Both Gerry and Tom were motivated to achieve, but not at any cost. Their friendship would proof to be very strong.

TWO

The hotel was situated on the corner of Main Street and Wallis Street, the frontage was long over 65 metres. It extended back through to Avery Lane about 70 metres towards the East. The hotel was in the shape of a U, with the open end facing Avery Lane. Along this side of the property was a wall providing privacy. The main entrance was on Main Street. The entry to the private bar was via the courtyard on Wallis Street through a door marked ladies bar. It could accommodate about 14 people, four at each of the three bigger tables and two in a small alcove to the side. It was in this nook of the private bar that Chap and George would meet in the evenings about once every six to eight weeks. There were dress rules for the private bar, no thongs, and shirts needed collars and sleeves. This ensured that most of the patrons used the public bar, leaving the private bar for more sedate encounters. This area had been redecorated by Teresa and Michelle soon after they took over the hotel. The seating was all made from warm New Guinea Rosewood, covered with maroon cushion. The walls were finished in a pale cream and the lighting was by way of ornate wall lamps. An artificial ceiling was installed to give the area a closeness about it, suggesting a feeling of intimacy. The dull lighting made it difficult to see who was using the cosy bar for a get together, a fact that Chap enjoyed, preferring to remain unnoticed. Chap was not really antisocial, he just disliked crowds of more than two. Chap was said to come from the big city and had engaged in other, local philanthropic gestures in the past. He seemed to have a very good understanding of finance, and enjoyed a challenge. It was thought that in years gone by, he must have had connections to Emerald.

He was known to very few. Chap was completely bald and appeared to have a deformity of the jaw as his left cheek was swollen and he spoke slowly as if in pain. This was thought to be the reason for his reclusive behaviour. George brought him a single Johnny Walker Black Label with a straw and a beer for himself and sat in the seat opposite Chap. He enquired about George's family, and how they were taking to the new way of life. George explained "life now, was very different, to what it used to be. While George and his sons were out fishing, there was always the fear that they might not, return from the sea. Now life moved at a more leisurely pace, with none of that worry. Teresa and Michelle were happy running their side of the business, dealing with people wanting accommodation for a while, to rest and recuperate. Each patron had their own story, but all agreed, it was good to get away from the rat race, which was the big city. Emerald was becoming well known amongst holiday makers, and quite a few reserved accommodation for the next year at the time of their departure." This showed they had to be doing something right. They believed a big smile on contact, worked miracles. Emerald was an average size town, and did not wish to embrace the impersonal approaches of the big city. It needed to be known as a holiday resort renowned for it's hospitality.

George showed Chap the figures for the past year and "he was happy with the slow but steady improvement in the turnover over each period of three months." They spoke about getting some painting done in the lounge, foyer and four of the bedrooms which were vacant at this time of year. It was agreed that the idea was sound and George should go ahead with this while things were quiet. Chap took the time to say " George was doing a very good job, and would reap the rewards." They discussed the possibilities for further improvements, and decided to wait for another three months, before looking at the situation again. Chap left after finishing his Johnny Walker drink, and disappeared into the night. George was very grateful for Chap's interest in the business. It had the effect of motivating George to try harder to improve their standing in the hotel industry. At present many of their ideas came from what they would expect as holiday makers arriving at the hotel.

Both George and Teresa knew, before making the decision to leave the sea and go into the hospitality industry, that it would be very stressful and risky. They believed they had little choice as the children were growing up fast, and they needed more stability and opportunities for their future. One of the biggest benefits of buying the hotel when they did, was it took place in the off season, between mid-winter and the spring break. So they had three months to get a feel of the business. The Christmas period and mid-winter, were the busiest times followed by Easter and the spring break.

To be honest there was no future in the fishing

industry. Their fishing operation was not big enough to support the family much longer. Although their boat was reasonably big, to progress they would either need a bigger boat, or a second boat and that was not practical. The fishing areas available could never justify that expansion. The beauty of the situation now was, the three children were old enough to make some sound suggestions, and in doing so created a more close-knit family striving for success. They all realised that this new venture was their life line. Teresa and Michelle had already, undertaken courses each year, through the Hotel Association on "Practical hotel Management" and had enrolled in further courses during the up coming, off season. Teresa regularly took a long look at the current menus, and discussed changes with the chef. One thing George made clear from day one was,there was no slate or "IOU system in operation. George had sent both Jack and Peter on courses related to dealing with the public, in situations where drink could be a factor. They both said this had given them good insight into how to defuse a situation with nobody feeling bad, or insulted. Dealing with an inebriated patron could be tricky as there was a shortage of logic, in one direction.

Four years prior George was looking to sell his

fishing boat and gear and get out of the fishing business as it was no longer as lucrative as it had been. He had a wife and three children and fishing was not going to give the children an edge in life. There were just too many restrictions on what to catch, when to catch it, and where to catch it. On top of that, the number of restricted areas had increased dramatically, over the past 10 years. When mentioning this to Gerry Keane, his tax consultant, George said he would have in excess of $1.5 million to put into some other form of business. He was hoping to be able to include his two sons, Jack and Peter in the new deal as they were his fishing crew. George stood 188cm tall and was pure muscle from all the hard physical work, he had put in at sea over the past 30 years. His sons Jack and Peter who were 18 and 17 respectively appeared to be from the same mould, as they were close behind in stature.

Gerry promised to keep his ears open for any possible opportunities. This Gerry did and he was sure that given the opportunity George would succeed. As over the time he had been doing George's tax he had got to know him as a hard working, disciplined and honest member of society. Some number of weeks later Gerry phoned George and said "there might be something in the wind.

Apparently the owner of one of the local hotels, on the north side, was going to sell up. His wife had been diagnosed with cancer, and it was thought she had little time to live. So they wanted to retire and concentrate on making life as easy as possible for her. The owner, who was completely devastated by the prognosis was keen for a quick sale. There being considerable concern as to how long she might live." This was not public knowledge yet so George should move quickly.

THREE

George reacted speedily to the news and contacted a local fellow, who had been pestering him to take over his boat and fishing quota. In the meantime George assembled the family and explained the situation. "The fishing business was no longer viable for them, the catch was getting smaller and the restrictions greater. There were five of them and each one was entitled to a life. They needed a business where they were all involved, so that they could push the turnover. Gerry was looking at a hotel and bar that was for sale and if they all agreed, then they could sell the boat and quotas, and go into that. He realised they had no experience but they were not stupid, and they knew how to work hard. Teresa and Michelle could run the hotel with casual labour, the boys and George could run the bar and off licence. They discussed this for a while, and finally agreed to go for the change. George said it would be difficult but if they pulled together they could do it." Arrangements were made to proceed with the hotel deal if George could get finance for the hotel. George phoned Gerry telling him,"he was ready to do business, if Gerry could find someone to loan him the shortfall." It was decided to offer the owner $2.1 million for a speedy sale. The hotel owner was happy to accept the offer for an immediate sale, as he was just keen to be free, to focus his attention on his wife's well- being.

Gerry was able to arrange the finances, at a very reasonable rate through a third party, a financial guru, a philanthropist from the big city. Being George's tax man, Gerry was able to provide a reference to the lender, Chap, that George was a worthwhile case and honest. The only proviso being the lender wished to meet regularly to see how things were going and to provide advice where necessary. Now, George was more than happy to have the advice of someone experienced in financial matters, so he gladly agreed to the idea. Arrangements were made, and George met Chap one evening in the very place they were sitting at now. Chap had a number of questions for George and he listened carefully to what George said in response. "Are you sure of the backing of your family"? Chap asked. To this George could honestly say "yes".

After a constructive session of questioning, Chap was satisfied that George realised what he was about to do would be taxing. All members of the family, would have to do their very best to pull together to make it work. Chap made it clear, that as they had no hotel experience he expected them to attend seminars on the industry, and how it works. He came away from the meeting comfortable that George and his family, had a good chance of achieving their dream. Gerry who had also done the hotel owners taxes knew the turnover of the hotel. He advised George that with his family on board they would be able to repay the debt in a reasonable time. Gerry said "The old financier, was about seeing people achieve something in their lives, as this was one of the few pleasures he could still enjoy. George could come and sign the application for the liquor licence the next day. It was very unlikely the application would be turned down," Gerry said. George and Teresa breathed a sigh of relief as they were aware that their fishing business was far from adequate for a family of five. The new venture would give them something to strive for. One important factor was that the three children respected their parents' decisions and would not engage in ridiculous arguments. This deal was sealed in a week, and the family approached their new venture with enthusiasm.

After a few months in the business it became clear to George, that the hotel was a very good purchase. The previous owner had been in a tight situation wanting to be rid of the hotel as soon as possible. He was obliged to take what he was offered as his wife's future was at stake. This played into George's hand as he could offer immediate cash. It became clear to George that the turnover was quite a bit higher than expected. As a result, George was able to up the repayments to reduce the time they would need, to pay the loan off. Gerry had looked after George's interests in the negotiations, and he would not forget it in a hurry. With George at the helm and his wife Teresa, two sons and daughter Michelle on board things were looking good. One of the advantages of the old hotel was there was private accommodation in the hotel for George and Teresa as well as a room for Michelle. Aside from the 10 double rooms in the main building, the annex provided a further five double rooms. The buildings had been kept in a good state of repair. This was a plus for the family as it meant they would not be spending large sums of money on maintenance in the short term. Jack and Peter could stay in the house, George owned and have their meals at the hotel. This suited George well as he had no desire to sell the house at present. If the boys were using the house it would be better looked after. If at a later date, house prices increased significantly, then they would reconsider their position. He knew things would change in time, but they would handle the issues as they arose.

Although the boys realised they did not need to be up early they were ready for the day by 7 am. It was not easy to sleep till 6am, if you have been used to getting up at 3am. Compared to crewing a fishing boat this was a breeze. The biggest issue was the way one treated the patrons, as they were always right. So a thorough inspection of the bar area as well as the facilities was done each morning. Ensuring all areas had been satisfactorily cleaned, well before opening time. Both the bar and the off licence had to be stocked up for the day. The two German Shepherd dogs, were taken for a run at 6 a.m. each morning along the beach by one of the boys. (They were free to roam around at night, to discourage anyone silly enough to contemplate a break in.) Once the daily routine was completed. They were able to sit down and discuss any issues relating to deliveries for the day, as well as any customer concerns. With guidance from Teresa they were able to provide some variety for pub lunches. This hands on approach had a subconscious effect on the patrons, who responded to the interest shown by George and his pleasant family. New faces started to appear with existing clients which made George and the boys feel they had the right approach. Darts and snooker competitions were encouraged, while provision was made for Domino players at one end of the bar.

Both Jack and Peter had played league for one of the local teams so their mates started frequenting "George's Pub" and soon their clientele had started to increase. George also had many fisherman friends from his 30 odd years in the trade. They now began to come to "George's Pub" for a drink and chat, knowing George would understand the issues, they were concerned about. There were many days when George would hear the complaints from the fishermen and think, "thank God I am out of it". The whole atmosphere became more friendly and sociable. Most of the time, George along with the two boys could handle the trade. There were a few incidents and usually the sight of George was more than enough, to get the aggressor to back down. One of the patrons that had caused a bit of trouble was Rodney Pleasant, who had drunk too much and became loud, abusive and obnoxious so he was banned for a month. Nipping bad behaviour in the bud was the best way to encourage patrons to enjoy themselves but also behave.

Terry Hegarty a senior constable in the Emerald Police, who lived on the north side, was a regular patron and he was always more than happy to help out behind the counter if required. It was good policy to have Terry as a patron, as this created a sense of belonging in Terry. This could be to their benefit should any police inspection be planned in the future. It was also a deterrent, ensuring things did not get out of hand. Two local teenagers helped with the beer kegs and the empties in the afternoons, if required. Teresa had two casuals, apart from the kitchen staff, who helped out most days ensuring the rooms were in order. A Further number of casuals were available at short notice should business pick up suddenly in the hotel. Either Teresa or Michelle would attend the reception area, ensuring the guests were well received. The pub was well patronised, by all sections of the community, both young and old. A few of the locals had been coming there for over 20 years, and they praised George for the way he was running the bar. Some played darts, others took to the snooker tables, while the domino fanatics zealously guarded their portion of the counter at the end of the bar.

George and Teresa were sitting having an early morning coffee, one Sunday and discussing the future of the family. "The hotel business was not really big enough for five adults," George said. "Once they had paid an appreciable portion of the loan. He would start looking around for another investment opportunity. The three children were getting good experience at the hotel and it would stand them in good stead in the future." He was impressed at the way Jack stepped in to take his place, if he was otherwise occupied. Maybe he could run a business, if they were lucky enough to find something in the next couple of years."

FOUR

Gerry Keane, was a local accountant and taxman, who with a partner, Mitchell Field, and a staff of five, ran a lucrative practise in upper Emerald. He had many interests in Emerald, having invested wisely since arriving in the town. Gerry did not enjoy the limelight, he preferred being unnoticed, but he was extremely gifted with an IQ in excess of 150, which placed him in a very small minority. His was definitely not a showman, he would listen to what was being discussed. Then if asked would share his thoughts but would certainly not try to run the topic of conversation. In some ways he appeared shy. He was quick on the uptake, but not one to force his ideas. He would rather listen than talk. He had a wide circle of acquaintances, but few real friends, in fact Tom was his best friend.

Since coming to Emerald he had completed a degree majoring in psychology and criminology. He had been responsible for implementing a local crime prevention program. Aiding the police by speaking to troublesome youths. On a one on one basis and giving them some advice. These contacts with the local youths had been helpful as they were more inclined to talk to Gerry than the police. Gerry's attitude and demeanour was so different to, that of the police that with minimum encouragement, he could get the teenagers to open up about their problems. He made no judgement of the youth, showed no animosity and was completely open when talking to them. Law enforcement was keen for him to continue this program.

Although Gerry was feeling his way in this new venture, he felt confident that they would be rewarded with positive results. Particularly now as they were using surf lifesaving as a tool, to stall the damaging practise of breaking and entering. Gerry ran every morning to remain fit and played squash twice a week at the local courts. He was a good swimmer but was not involved in lifesaving, preferring to concentrate on the youth needing help, with their approach to life.

One of the drawbacks of seaside towns, was the temptation for youth not to bother getting a job, but spend time at the beach. This practice was probably more prevalent in Emerald, because of the wonderful weather. This worked some of the time, like in the holiday periods when there were plenty of people around, and one could always be invited to join a group, enjoying some activity or other. The youth in general were drawn to the beach as it was "laid on" pleasure, just help yourself.

When things got tough, in the off season, when there was not much happening, the situation changed. No group to latch onto, no ready available food. Then it was time to visit the food stall in town, just prior to closing, asking for left overs. Sleeping rough was something one had to get used to, you needed a rug or two and some towels for a pillow. There was no money so one would have to nick, something worthwhile and try to sell it. Slowly the realisation that they were going nowhere fast, dawned on them. The problem seemed to be more common among the less fortunates, in society. Most parents expected their teenage children to either be studying, or have a job, if not they were on their own. Now there existed a couple of possibilities, one could become a runner for a drug supplier or you could go around to different businesses asking for work. Some tried to find jobs others decided being a runner was easier going.

So eventually the landscape changed some faces disappeared and new ones appeared. It was a cycle that Gerry was hoping to break. Maybe it should be addressed at school first, where the pupils might get the message. However there were always those that were not interested in the message, they would wait and see what became available. The thing was that at school you were a somebody, once you left school you were a nobody. If you had not made prior arrangements to start a trade with some firm, once you finished school and you were not going to university, then there was a vacuum that needed filling.

Spider was not his real name, what mother would call her son Spider? He came from a family of six children or more, he did not know how many. He remembered very little of his early childhood. In fact he did not care to remember it at all. His mother was the dominant figure. He had vague recollections of a male figure who would come, and go for extended periods. He learned early on to look after himself, as his mother had little time to do so. What with younger siblings, there was just so little time to go around, Being the eldest he would often lose out. So he learned to scrounge food from the food outlets and from people sitting along the seaside. Early on it became necessary to nick clothes, and shoes left lying around. It was amazing how people put down articles of clothing and did not come back to retrieve them.

He did not remember when he left home, in fact he was not born in Emerald and could not remember how he got there. It just happened like many things in Spider's life, he probably got a lift there and was late for the return run. He was not fazed. There was a nice beach here with plenty of sand dunes, it seemed a good place to be. He would hang around and find out how he could get along. He was okay with his situation now. He was free of the hassle of looking after the younger siblings. They were always wanting something. He had enough to do looking after himself, and avoiding the truancy inspector. Spider was not prone to emotion, he did what he had to do to survive. This was basically how he got along, but he would not be stood on. Although Spider claimed he did not remember his name or how he got to Emerald, this was probably a matter of convenience. He wished to forget the past and start again. He had no desire to return home to the whining siblings, he wished to be free of all that. He would hangout near fast food outlets, in the late afternoons and get a plastic bag of discarded food, and head down to the sand dunes. He spent a fair bit of time down there, keeping out of the way of adults, digging hollows in the sand to avoid the biting winds. In the early mornings he liked to go for a long run on the beach, stretching himself to see if he could go further than the day before. Early on, Spider realised he would have to learn to fight, to keep his position in the hierarchy that existed in this strange world of misfits. If somebody wanted a towel or pair of sneakers that you had, then it was up to you to defend your possessions. If you lost the fight, you lost your possession as well. He managed to nick towels on the beach, as well as rugs to make himself a comfortable place to sleep. He claimed he had no idea of when his birthday was, or how old he was, not even his name. To Spider these things were not important, staying alive and finding food was. So he conveniently forgot his past.

He remembered an older boy (Rick) coming up to him one day and saying he would pay him to do little jobs for him. The older boy asked him his name and he just said the first thing that came into his head, "Spider" so he became known by this name. He could not recall his real name and anyway it did not matter. He had no idea at this time, what the little parcels contained only that he got paid 50 cents for every parcel that he delivered. He knew he could count to 10, the same as the fingers on his hands. He soon got to know the smell of these little parcels, and one of the other runners told him it was weed. So he wanted payment after every 10, parcels of weed.

It was not usually far that he had to go, he was just told not to be seen handing over the parcel, he had no idea why. He found it strange that Rick was too lazy to do his own deliveries.

On the street one had to learn quickly how things worked or else you suffered. Spider was given a certain area to cover with his deliveries, and he soon learned who his customers were. Giving a parcel to the wrong customer, could get you beaten up. Slowly his working area became larger, and Spider started saving money, he did not need to spend. Why buy something if you can nick it. Life was tough out there, but when you did not know any different, you knuckled down, and did what you had to. One day he was doing a delivery, when he saw a boy standing around that he did not recognise. The stranger confronted him, and Spider said it was his turf, and he did no have to ask permission to be there. So the bigger boy laid into Spider, giving him a beating, but Spider did not cry. Spider returned to

Rick telling him what happened, and that the bigger guy took his parcel.

"Okay you go back the same way you did before, and I will come around the other side of the block, and let us see what he says this time" Rick said. Spider did as he was told and he could see the same boy standing where Spider had left him. Spider carried on walking towards him, and he saw Rick come up behind the imposter, and before he could challenge Spider, Rick laid into the imposter, giving him a belting and sending him on his way, telling him not to return. This taught Spider two things, you don't back down, and you give your adversary a hiding to remember. So Spider was developing a narcissistic attitude in his endeavours to stay alive. Maybe he was born with this trait, and he was just strengthening it as he strived to get ahead. Spider was not big, he was thin maybe a little tall for his age, but what he needed to do was get fit and learn how to defend his patch. Spider started doing exercises in the mornings to give himself some strength, and slowly he became a little heavier. From what he could see the best way to attack, was to just throw fists as hard and fast as possible, until the opposition crumbled. Spider was learning his "trade" as quickly as he could. He wanted to be top dog. There were few places that could boast they did not have a drug problem. A druggie would stoop to any level to get a fix, and Spider was more than willing to provide the stimulant.

FIVE

Gerry had been asked to stand for council, but felt he could not fill the roll of a talker, and was of more use doing what he was doing now. Bev, Gerry's wife who was a dress designer, ran a dress boutique in north Emerald, employing two seamstresses. Bev and Gerry had a daughter Jane who was a pupil at the local primary school. Jane although only 9 years of age showed ability far beyond her years on the violin. Bev and Gerry were very impressed with her playing and eagerly encouraged her. The Keanes lived on the North side of town on a beautiful property studded with big pine trees down the west side, giving lovely shade in the afternoons. The home was a three bedroom, study and sun room, brick structure with tiled roof. The surrounding lawns, and flower beds were maintained by a gardener. On the left side of the home was a patio with a barbecue, ready to be used.

The home was one street from the north side of the lake, in a desirable part of town, and some evenings Gerry, Bev and Jane would walk along the edge of the lake enjoying the sunset. This was a very quiet and peaceful part of north Emerald.

A bridge, over the estuary, of the lake joined north and south Emerald. The town of Emerald, with a population of 75 odd thousand, was situated on the east coast roughly 350 kilometres north of the big city. Four times a year it was inundated with holiday makers boosting the population to well over 200,000. So in order to accommodate this influx, there were 11 high rises, with fancy apartments, as well as many hotels, motels, a myriad of houses, flats, caravan parks, and camping areas available to help relieve the cashed up visitors of their money. The younger crowd were keen on camping as it was by far the cheapest option, so they made full use of the 14 camping sites in the shire, and some partook of the weed available. Emerald had a beautiful climate, hot summers and winters with cool nights and wonderful sunny days. At these times people were everywhere, some on the lake, others sitting along the terrace, enjoying the sun. There would be people skiing on the lake, while others were on a hire fishing boat on their way out to sea to catch the big one. Restaurants would be full of patrons, some enjoying breakfast while others were having morning tea, or early brunch. When the town was this full of people the police and emergency services, including surf lifesavers had to be on full alert, as they could be called out to any number of places across this vast region.

Four times a year trade was brisk in Emerald whether you were providing, accommodation, oysters,hiring out tinnies, fishing boats or cruises on the lake, not to mention providing local cuisine at any number of restaurants. Swimming gear was in big demand, as could be vouched for by Shirley Edwards, the manager of one of the leading clothing and sportswear stores. Shirley was married to Tom Edwards, a local businessman, who owned "Edwards Security" a firm specialising in commercial, industrial and domestic security. Tom was a qualified electrical engineer,who came up to Emerald after completing his studies. Looking for a town, where the surfing was good, and the climate just right. Tom was just glad to get out of the big city, and live life at a more sane pace. Emerald suited his wants, and he settled, starting Edwards Security and joined the lifesavers. At first Tom would go around visiting the small businesses and home owners explaining what he was capable of delivering, and how he went about it. Soon the Security business was attracting interest, and once the people became aware of how conscientious Tom was, and how well his systems worked, the business flourished. Soon the bigger businesses were becoming interested in the idea of installing security to protect their wares as break ins were very costly. It did not matter how big or small a town was, there were always those that would break into homes, or businesses and create havoc, misery and a feeling of insecurity. A number of large companies in the big city had huge warehouses in Emerald from which products would be drawn a couple of times a week. The logic being that it was much cheaper to have a safe warehouse there and draw from it as required than have a very expensive facility in the big city subject to frequent break- ins. These warehouses could be protected by one of Tom's systems. So the industrial area was increasing in size as the businesses realised they would be better off with a facility in Emerald. Non perishable items could be stored and could be delivered to the big city in a matter of just over three hours, allowing the company to operate from a smaller shop front.

In the industrial division, there was a large lit

area, where semi-trailers were able to park for 12 hours to give the drivers time to sleep. Right next to it, was a 24 hour complex with filling station, ablution block and eatery where the drivers were able to take care of their needs before continuing on the final leg of their run. Down the east coast, Emerald was the second stop for the long haul truckies bringing produce down to the big city from up north. In this area, Tom had installed cameras to provide surveillance on the trucks, while the owners slept. It was essential to provide the truckies, with a sense of security for themselves, and their laden rigs. Emerald businesses knew that to protect the business they had, it was essential to be proactive. The truckies knew they were well looked after here at Emerald, so the stop was always well patronized. The site was about 1 kilometre off the highway so it did not add much to the travel time.

The four technicians that worked for Tom were now trained up to his standard. These men were capable of installing home systems, and ones for small businesses. On the bigger jobs, Tom would have to design them, and oversee the installation, and commissioning. Tom and his men had pagers, and they had a roster system with one of them being on call every fifth week. Tom included himself in this programme. To show his employees his involvement and commitment, and most of all to keep his finger on the pulse. Now the security business was doing well, Tom was seriously thinking of starting a solar power, installation company. He had discussed the idea with Gerry who had listened to the pros and cons. Gerry believed that on the presentation Tom made to him, it was a sound idea. Tom was very pleased with Gerry's assessment of the situation, and was planning to go ahead with his scheme.

The senior lifeguards including Tom were engaged in the training of the young lifesavers. This took place early on Saturday mornings as well as Tuesday and Thursday afternoons after school. When, two lifesavers, who were tradies and finished work at 3 pm. would put the boys through their paces. Tom got great pleasure from watching the young boys develop physically, improve their swimming, and become proficient as lifesavers. This boded well for the future of lifesaving, in the Emerald region. With the area so big, it required a large number of lifesavers, but these were dedicated men devoted to protecting swimmers from the dangers of the sea. The task of a lifesaver, was an onerous one, and sometimes it was possible to become despondent, as the swimmers appeared to be their own worst enemies. The lifesavers on duty had to check the beaches for currents or rifts, as they decided whether or not the beach would be safe for the public. The flags would then be positioned and a lifesaver kiosk along with the kit would be put in place and manned. However there were always those that ignored the flags, going for a swim when inebriated, or swimming at night. The only way to look at it, is we are all human and make mistakes. The holiday makers, do not know the local beaches like the lifesavers do, hence the mistakes. Most of the time swimming outside the flags was an honest mistake, and the swimmer would immediately comply. It did not take long for Tom to meet Shirley in the surfing fraternity, and they started dating. Tom was not as extroverted as Shirley but they seemed to like many of the same things. Shirley had a friend Eli, whom she had known since starting school, and they were best friends, so it was inevitable that Tom would meet her very soon.

Often on their casual outings Shirley would ask Tom, if Eli could come along as she was all alone, Tom was more than happy to have her there, as he enjoyed her company. All of them liked the outdoors and a laid back life, when not at work. They surfed together, swam together and enjoyed going on

Tom's boat. Slowly it appeared Tom and Shirley were getting serious about each other, so Eli backed off a bit, to give them air. However she would still see Shirley every day and most lunchtimes. After two years Tom and Shirley were married and Eli was the bridesmaid. The ceremony was held in Tom's garden under the beautiful big fig tree,where a marriage celebrant officiated. It was a small wedding, with, Don, Gerry, Bev and Jane as well as, friends from karate, and lifesaving. All entering into the spirit of the occasion, having a jolly good time. Enjoying the beautifully presented eats and drinks in the barbecue area. Caterers were brought in for the occasion, as it was the most practical method for the celebration. Tom and Shirley spent two weeks on honeymoon at Seaview, a small coastal town about 100 kilometres North of Emerald. The two were very happy together.

One day Spider was walking along when a fellow approached him questioning his right, to be where he was, and he gave a good account of himself, sending the fellow packing. The next occasion some guy came along and demanded Spider's sneakers. Spider immediately got stuck into this fellow, giving him a good belting for his cheek. Slowly Spider was becoming more street wise. Spider gained confidence in his abilities, he also started noticing other things happening on the streets. He saw men cruising in cars stopping to talk to women, and then picking them up and driving off. He was not sure what that was about, but he reckoned he would find out in time. Rick had told him to be wary of the police driving around as they made trouble. In a police car they were easy to see but in an unmarked car it was different.

He was grabbed by a policeman in plain clothes one day. Fortunately for him, he was too quick for the policeman to see him, discard the little package. Once he had heard the lecture and the policeman went off, he retrieved the weed. Spider began to recognise the unmarked police cars and took his time to make sure he would not be caught by them. By now Spider understood he was a runner for a drug distributor, and he was okay with that. Spider had not tried weed yet, as he knew he had to be aware of his surroundings. He had to have a good grasp of how everything fitted in place. At this time he approached Rick and said he was Rick's best runner, and he felt he needed an increase, as he had been doing it for over four years now without losing any parcels. Rick considered the situation with Spider, and he had to admit he was at work everyday, and did his job well. He had alerted Rick twice to strangers trying to infiltrate their area, so he was worth keeping, so he told Spider he would put him up to 60 cents for every parcel of weed delivered. This was more like it now he could save some money.

Spider was looking for a place to stay where he was protected from the rain. At present his home made swag was getting wet, too often. When he was not running for Rick he walked around the neighbourhood looking for an old building he could use. It must have been a few weeks later he was up at the north end of Emerald. He saw a property with two old houses on it, and it had a fence he could creep through. He went in to look around, and there seemed to be a couple of places he could use to keep dry. It was not that far from where he usually operated, and it would be nice to have a dry swag for a change. The next day after his last run, he loaded his things on a bicycle, he borrowed from Terry. One of the runners he got on with, and took his kit up to his new digs. It took a while to get settled and feel comfortable there. It really was much better than sleeping under the lifesavers building, or in amongst the dunes.

There were other advantages. He found various

places he could hide his possessions. The money, he put in limited amounts in each place so as not to loose it all at once. At least this way he could check to see if it was disappearing. He had a long dagger that he could not carry on him, so he found a place to hide it. Two knives he hid separately, believing someone finding one knife would probably not look for a second one. He did not believe anybody could possibly find all his treasures. So all in all he had at least a dozen places to keep his things safe. In order to see if anybody visited the house, in his absence. He strung a line of thread between a couple of doorways when he left in the morning. Spider believed if he could improve his turnover he could eventually become a big dealer. He could then have people under him that did the dirty work, and he could be someone important. He first needed to be seen as someone that could be trusted by the dealer. He had ideas of overthrowing a dealer at some time in the future.

Tom and Shirley had a lovely property on the south side, close to one mile beach, where the land blocks were still a reasonable size. There was a huge fig tree on the south west side of the property providing wonderful shade in the afternoons. Tom had his boat and cars undercover leaving plenty of space for his barbecue area. As it was light from 4.30 am. in the summer months they could go down for a swim early in the morning. Get home, have breakfast and be at work on time. Since moving to Emerald, Tom had built up a sound business and he was proud of what he had done. He was established now and had the majority of the business in the region. Tom had strict work ethics, and refused to ignore these. They were the foundation of his business, and he tried to instil this attitude in his staff. In big businesses the security was more complex, and warnings were provided to the local police for attention. In a couple of instances thieves have tried to gain entry to big warehouses, only to have the police there in a matter of minutes. Home systems were not that complex, and a call in to the firm would alert the serviceman on duty to pay a visit. In the case of home calls, it was usually as a result of the owner moving, some item of furniture that has broken the beams signal, resulting in a call out. The roster system Tom had introduced gave each employee four weeks off, and one week on. Tom planned to expand the business over the coming months.

Shirley and Tom were married but, alas, had no children. Shirley had been for numerous tests, and Tom's sperm count had been checked. Over the years they had, had every test possible, but to no avail. For whatever reason their reproductive systems, did not produce the desired result. Shirley was tired of it all, and felt a little hard done by. However she knew that was no way to approach life. She was a clever girl who had done remarkably well. Having taken over the management of her father's business very successfully. There were other things in life that one could concentrate on, Taekwondo, lifesaving, friendships and being a better person. Shirley was a faithful wife and had strong principles about marriage. Tom had accepted the doctor's results and moved on. He and Shirley had a good life here in Emerald, and now it depended on them to show what they were capable of. Tom would concentrate on the things he was good at, lifesaving and growing his businesses. Shirley was good at lifesaving too, and she was ready to compete for her black belt in Taekwondo, a Korean art of self defence. Shirley got onto the committee to encourage visitors to Emerald. So the idea to make Emerald an attractive destination, took hold. Since then three members of the committee spent two days each year, down in the big city promoting the region. So Shirley and Tom turned a negative into a positive, make Emerald "the place to be" became their slogan.

What many people did not realise, was that the region was very big. To get around the area one needed a vehicle and a four wheel drive would probably be the best option. There were some beaches that were open to four wheel drive vehicles, and others that could only be accessed by a four wheel drive vehicle. Tom and Shirley had swum at most of the beaches, but were happy where they were, with easy access to one mile beach. This was not to say that you could not have a wonderful time with a two wheel drive vehicle, on the contrary, many people have no desire to drive on a beach or off road. The local facilities extended over many kilometres, included 11 beaches, numerous camping sites, and fishing areas both on the lake and out at sea. The lake which covered over 98 square kilometres, served as a recreational area, as well as an oyster farm, and people could be found enjoying the serenity of the lake, any time of the day or night. On the north east side of the lake there were 4 beautiful big fig trees providing shade. For those interested in resting a while. It had a wonderful relaxing effect on all, who decided to spend time there. The area was very popular with locals and visitors alike. People from the big city were very impressed by the calming effect of the surroundings and were happy to just sit, and enjoy it.

The oyster growers were confined to the east and north shallows, of the lake. Other water activities were spread out over the rest of the lake. A little way down on the East Side of the lake, people could buy oysters fresh out of the water. The oyster farming in this area was quite intensive. Charter boats for deep sea fishing were available for hire, which included the skipper. As there was a shifting sand bank, at the estuary of the lake, this needed to be negotiated very carefully, and the skippers knew the best areas to catch fish. There were three rivers flowing into the lake which maintained its natural water level. So the area influenced by the tides, was largely around the estuary. The lake, with an average depth of about two and a half metres, was a huge attraction. A boat regularly took groups of visitors on the lake and these trips were often accompanied by dolphins swimming at the bow of the boat, providing much excitement for the patrons. Pleasure craft pulled skiers around and people sunbathed on the beautiful white sand banks protruding from the waters at low tide, on the edges of the lake. Life was good!

Shirley was a very attractive lady with blonde hair, blue eyes and a good figure that she kept in trim with Taekwondo. She had been doing for over

10 years, and was planning to go for her black belt, in the next month. However there was much more to Shirley, she was not boastful. Since the first day of school, at meeting Eli, she soon realised Eli was alone. There was nobody looking after her. Her mother was busy running an evening cleaning business and her father was never around. Shirley instinctively took over the task as her friend and mentor. As well she had been involved with surf lifesaving, since her early teens when her father introduced her to it. Twice a week Tom and Shirley did lifesaving practice and once a week Shirley did Taekwondo,with Eli. Both Tom and Shirley worked hard during the week so they relaxed with their friends Eli, Gerry and Bev Keane on the week ends.

Shirley managed the store her dad, Don Williams had started some 34 years earlier. The store was well positioned in Head Lane where it had been since Don first opened it's doors, all those years ago. The business had always done well as Don and Shirley strived to keep the various articles of swimwear and casual wear, pertinent to the latest trends. Swimwear and towels were in demand all day long, as well as, some form of headgear to protect against the sun. Most days Don would be in the office, at the back of the store helping where he could. His wife,

Shirley's mum, had died of cancer two years back, and Don was at a loose end most days, when not playing bowls. Shirley was very happy to have her father close by, as she did not see him that much over the weekends. Shirley's elder brother, was an engineer, who lived in England.

Tom had a seven metre boat with two 200hp motors which was more than adequate to pull two skiers around on the lake. Tom,Gerry, Shirley and Eli were very good skiers while Bev, Gerry's wife, was happy to be on the lake with her friends. Piloting the boat when the others were busy. On the north side of the lake, on the seaward side of the bridge, there was anchorage for the local fishermen and the fisherman's co-op, was right there, ready to receive the daily catch. The chandler,s store was over the road from the co-op, in the first street up from the quays. The fishermen and their crews went out about 3 - 4 in the morning. They would arrive back from about 11am, depending on how good the fishing was. Some of the public would descend on the co-op to buy fresh fish. While others wanted fish, and chips to eat at the tables outside on the deck, and enjoy the beautiful surroundings. Further down towards the estuary, was an enclosed beach. Here the mothers would bring their younger children, to play in the water, safely. On the opposite side of the estuary, in the distance one could see the coastguards lookout station. Where the coastguards were keeping an eye out for boats getting into strife, and needing help. This was indeed a very beautiful part of the east coast.

SIX

Natalie Stokes was an attractive young lady with red hair, who lived with her mum in a council house in north Emerald. She had left school at 15 and got a job, to help support her mum whose arthritis, was steadily becoming more crippling. She had undertaken a secretarial course at Tafe after hours, while working at the local supermarket as a "check out chick." Now she was working as a secretary to Rodney Pleasant, a lawyer, and a very nasty piece of work. Rodney was not true to his name, he was often inebriated, quite rude, bad tempered and lacked any respect for the opposite sex. He had offices above a chemist shop in north Emerald. These offices were no more than a reasonably sized room, with a division across the middle creating two smaller rooms. The division was made of wood panelling at the lower half, and frosted glass above.

Here Natalie, who started at 8 30am, ran the

office, attended to telephone enquiries, potential clients at the door and all correspondence. Rodney would turn up at about 9 am, often unshaven and attend to any paperwork, that was left on his desk by Natalie for signature, and any other matters. Then, in an abrupt manner, (he was always abrupt when he had a raging thirst) he would instruct her about any correspondence that needed her attention, that day. After which he would say he was off to court, and slam the door on his way out. His first port of call being "George's Pub" where he had a shot of vodka, followed by a beer. Once he felt he could face his world, he would visit the public prosecutors, and the courts seeing what business he could drum up. From day one Rodney did not treat Natalie well. He was loud mouthed, often drunk and swore at her about things that were none of her concern. Some of this treatment was possibly due to the fact, that Natalie had made it clear from day one, that she would not tolerate any of his advances. She had a big uncle who would sort him out if he persisted. (There was no uncle but it did have the desired effect.) After two years of this treatment Natalie thought she had enough experience, to apply for a better job so she decided to find other employment. She had applied for a couple of positions advertised, in the local newspaper, and had been for two interviews.

The second one was with Gerry Keane, who was looking for a replacement secretary, as one of his assistants was moving interstate. Natalie asked for an interview, after hours, as she knew Rodney would be very reluctant to give her time off. He would want to know what it was for, and Natalie was not about to tell him. Natalie attended Gerry's offices, which were in walking distance on the north side. Gerry, who had a casual disarming manner, could see that although Natalie's C.V. showed only two years of experience as a secretary. She had attended Tafe for two years, after hours, to get her secretarial diploma, all while working full time, to accomplish this. Which showed someone with tenacity and drive. This was in conflict with what the young lady sitting in front of him portrayed, she appeared downcast, apprehensive and a little withdrawn.

Gerry, noticing Natalie's demeanour, started slowly, speaking to her gently and explained what he was looking for. Gerry gradually got her to open up about her up bringing and how her father walked out on them, when she was just six years old, and how she left school at 15 so she could go to work to help her mother, she being the only child. When pushed, Natalie broke down, and said "She had a very stressful time working for Rodney, as he had no respect for her as an individual and a woman. He shouted and swore at her, as if it was quite normal conduct. The only reason she had put up with this abuse, was because she wanted some appreciable time on her C.V. as it was her first job." Rodney had an unenviable reputation in town of being vindictive, abusing and swearing at those who he believed crossed him, especially when he had drink in him.

This disclosure, by Natalie, fitted in with what Gerry had come to believe, knowing some of what Rodney was capable of. Gerry decided to offer Natalie the position in his firm as he saw definite potential in her. She had quite a bit of experience in a lawyer's office, and showed tenacity by staying in the job for two years in spite of Rodney's ill treatment. He explained that she would have to serve a probationary period of three months. Once that was over, and both Gerry and Natalie were satisfied with the situation then, Natalie would be on permanent staff and would receive an increase in salary. Natalie accepted immediately, as it was obvious to her that working conditions would be much better than what she had experienced, working for Rodney. Gerry said "I will ask one of the secretaries to type a letter of appointment, in the morning. Could Natalie return the following afternoon, to sign it?" Natalie agreed to return the next afternoon to sign it after work, to start in one month's time. Natalie returned the next afternoon after work, and signed the letter of appointment in Gerry's office. Before she left Gerry told her "If you had any trouble with Rodney when you give notice, contact me immediately." Gerry would be much more than a match for Rodney, Natalie thought. She noticed she was starting at a salary $30 dollars a month more than what she was getting now. Natalie would have been happy to start at the same miserable salary, Rodney was paying her. Gerry who had strong work ethics, believed in paying employees a decent wage, and keeping them happy. As he knew from experience that not looking after them would result in discontented employees, keen to look for greener pastures. Over the years Gerry was proud to say he had a very stable, and efficient office staff.

Spider made himself at home in the old house, but he was cautious to leave the house before it was light and to return after dark. He nicked a battery operated lamp that he could use when he had covered the windows. So no one could see a light inside at night. The places where he had hidden his precious things seemed to be okay, as to date nothing had disappeared which he found reassuring. Judging by the threads he had put in place, at some of the doorways he did not believe anybody had been snooping around there. However he got the impression that there was a living owner, who could not or did not care too much, about looking after his assets. Some parts of the fencing were simply held together by short pieces of tie wire. In other places it looked as if the weeds had been sprayed with weedkiller. Maybe the owner was very old, so he could only do a little in the way of repairs at one time. Spider was beginning to feel comfortable in his new digs, he just made sure he was not seen entering or leaving the property. Rick had quite a few runners but Spider did not know how many. He did believe he was probably the longest serving runner. Rick called him one morning, and said that because he had been with Rick some time, he would give Spider the chance to deliver smack.

Now Spider, did not have the vaguest idea what smack was he just said sure. Spider was happy with the promotion, and asked what the delivery price was. Rick said for every parcel of smack he would get one dollar. The most important issue with smack was, not to get caught with it on you. The police would have a field day if they caught a runner with smack. The harassment and intimidation was relentless, with threats of a long jail term. Then they would say, if the runner gave up the name of the dealer they might go easy on him. So Spider would deliver either weed or smack, but he could not be fooled. He could smell weed, and also feel the contents of the parcels were different so he could work out his wages. Spider never forgot those words about being caught with smack. Spider was building himself a nice little nest egg with his earnings, as he spent little money in his day. If he needed shoes he knew where he could nick a good pair from a shop nearby. He still made a habit of going to the takeaways at closing time hoping to get some leftovers. Spider decided it was not wise to have just one place where he could stay as it was too predictable for anybody watching him. So he obtained boarding with Mrs. Mathews in the old boarding house. Mrs. Mathews was an elderly lady who rented out rooms to supplement her old age pension. Now he could stay at the old house or at Mrs. Mathews depending on which place suited him, on the day.

All the time Spider was watching Rick to see how he operated, he moved his location and would hide his supplies in different places, so that if someone thought they could rip him off they would be unsuccessful. It seemed Rick got his supplies after dark as Spider had never seen supplies delivered. The way the system worked was, a punter went along to where the dealer traded, and paid for whatever goods he wanted. Then a runner would deliver the product to the punter's hangout. This reduced the likelihood of losing the money, and the product. It also ensured the punter did not see where the product was kept, thus preventing a raid by the punter. As time went on Spider reckoned he was right to run his own outfit. He was about 19 and had 10 years experience in the drug trade. The question was how was he going to go about it. He knew all the runners in the group he served but he was not pally with them. Spider would have to bide his time, he was sure the opportunity would present itself. Spider continued his delivery of the products bought without any major incidents, but he was very careful. He had absolutely no intention of getting caught with smack on him. Those words of warning about the smack were forever in his memory, and he was never caught with smack. However Spider had been inside the police cells on at least nine occasions for pedalling drugs, usually weed. Further he had been up for assault three times, when he got carried away beating someone up.

Natalie went home very excited to tell her mother about the job offer from Mr. Keane and showed her the letter confirming her position with "Keane and Associates". "I am very proud of what you have done and achieved", her mum said. Life was looking up. She and her mum sat chatting about how this would help to ease their financial situation a little. The next morning at work Natalie did not say anything to Rodney as she was only required to give two weeks notice. The time seemed to go so slowly now, that she knew she was leaving. Eventually the time came for Natalie to hand in her letter of resignation. Well, as expected, Rodney had plenty to say.

On opening Natalie's letter of resignation, Rodney exploded, saying Natalie was disloyal, downright inconsiderate and underhand. Under no circumstances would he provide her with a reference, as her work was mediocre at best. Natalie survived this horrific onslaught by thinking positively about her future, and ignoring all the foul language. Quite frankly Natalie already had a job, and she certainly did not need a reference from Rodney. The atmosphere was strictly icy for the term of her notice, which seemed to last forever, but eventually Natalie left unscathed and very relieved.

During the time of her notice, Natalie overheard Rodney telling a lady, Estelle Brown, by name, in his office that he was sure they could find some other form of payment. As he had an immediate appointment if she came back, after five o'clock he would be able to help her. Natalie knew that this statement was not true, as he had no further appointments that day. If he had she would have knowledge of them or it would be in his diary, but there was nothing and it puzzled Natalie. Rodney was not one to work overtime so she decided to lay a trap, believing Rodney was up to no good. Prior to knocking off that afternoon she took the office recording machine, as Rodney had shown her on more than one occasion. Placed it on the small cabinet against the dividing partition in her office. She then stuck the pencil shaped recording microphone through the small hole in the panel so it was in amongst some artificial flowers on the cabinet in Rodney's office. She went into Rodney's office to make sure the microphone was not visible and returned to her office, and set the recorder in motion and left the premises.

Next morning Natalie got to work a bit earlier, and reclaimed the recorder and played back what she had recorded the previous afternoon. She heard herself closing the office door and then it was quiet for about 10 minutes. Then Rodney returned and a few minutes later Mrs Brown arrived. Rodney ushered her into his office, and when seated Rodney asked her what was worrying her. She proceeded to explain her concerns. Estelle had caught her husband having an affair, and she wished to take him to court, and divorce him. As she was sick and tired of his carrying on with other women, but she was unable to pay at the moment as her husband had emptied their joint bank account. Rodney explained to the Mrs. Brown that he was sure they would come to an equitable solution as money, was not the only way the costs could be defrayed, so they should proceed with the paperwork and he would get the process in motion as these things take time. She should not worry herself any further.

Natalie knowing Rodney, realised where this was going, stopped the recorder and removed the tape putting it in her handbag. Remembering what Gerry had said to her about letting him know if Rodney was unpleasant she decided she would give the tape to Gerry when she started working there, believing Gerry would know what to do with it.

While Spider was considering how he could

likely overthrow Rick's position as leader of the group, he had some good fortune. Rick was arrested by the cops for beating his wife savagely, as well as the guy he caught her in bed with. They were both transported to Eden hospital in a very serious condition. To make matters worse Rick was caught with four parcels of smack on him. Now this altered the situation considerably, with regard to the charges of assault there were extenuating circumstances. He could get two years for that, but being caught with four lots of smack at 5gms each, this was considered serious, and he would receive a minimum of three years possibly more.

Spider happened to be on his way to Rick to collect an order, when he saw this operation go down. Realising that this was serious, he waited for his opportunity, went into Rick's den collected all the drugs and removed himself from the site before the cops could get there for a thorough search. Spider let it be known that he was in charge now, and all business would be done through him. Of the nine runners, one contested this decision, but not for long, he was dispatched after a sound beating. Among the drugs etc. that Spider found in Ricks den was a number apparently for the supplier. So Spider phoned, telling them what happened, and that he was now running the show. They had obviously heard his name before as they did not query the statement, and told him where they would meet him for the next delivery. This first delivery he received, without any down payment, but any subsequent delivery would have to be paid for immediately. Spider quickly got the hang of things, and decided he needed another two runners. Within half a day his needs were met, and he started pushing the boundaries of his operation.

The biggest part of pushing drugs was to never look as if you were doing so. Be fully aware of your surroundings as well as who is coming and who is going. If a new face appears then you need to know why. The runners had the knack of being unseen in full sight, they might be playing basketball against a wall, they may be riding a bicycle, playing dice or walking by. When the action was necessary, then they were there. The money for a street kid was good, all he had to do was deliver something, without being seen. This required that he knew his territory very well, but that was no big deal, this was where he lived, and it was like being free. Contact with the dealer was by way of a throw away mobile. He would phone the runner and say he had a parcel for delivery.

It was about this time that Spider started sampling the product, and he liked the way he felt. Marijuana made him feel good, just floating, but still in control. He did not want to do something stupid, and lose his business, so he smoked one zoll when he relaxed at night. He also decided as a business man he needed a surname, so he would be known as Spider Kelly, he had seen the name on a tyre at the local service station, and thought it sounded good. A man in his position should have a surname, preferably one that sounded good, and Kelly sounded just right. Another issue he had was it would be more practical for him to get around if he had a car. However Spider did not have a driver's licence for a car. This would necessitate him using one of his pushers who had a car, as his driver. He did not like this idea but it would have to do for the present. As soon as he could find a full time driver he would use him. It was necessary to visit the runners to see all was good, and to re enforce the fact that he was in charge.

Spider was enjoying his new position of importance, and with it seemed to come a more aggressive disposition, towards those who crossed him. He had started having a zoll in the morning as well as the evening and this might have been the cause of his rage. Any individual causing him displeasure was sure to get a beating he would not forget. Business was thriving but somehow it did not make Spider's temper any better. He was known as a local enforcer, if someone wished to score one over another individual, and this came at a price. Maybe he believed he needed to be more aggressive to discourage any would be opposition. Whatever the reason was, Spider made his displeasure obvious to all concerned. At this time Spider was making very good money with his operation, as the markup on drugs was huge because of the possibility of getting caught.

SEVEN

Gerry, since completing his degree in psychology and criminology had not been idle. He had continued his interest in both fields with drugs and alcohol as factors in our lives. He was of the opinion that, in life there is a light side and a dark side, for each of us. Some of us seem unaware of this as their lives are lived on the light side, without ever experiencing the terrible dangers of the dark side, and the consequences thereof. Others venture onto the fringes of this awful abyss, and quickly shy away feeling tainted and uncomfortable. Then there are those who enjoy moving over to the dark side with others on occasion, tempting fate, never realising the awful danger they are exposing themselves to. They are keen to return to the light side. Others frequent the dark side, more often either unaware of the dangers involved or believing they are safe. Those that imagine that visiting the dark side is without peril are in for a rude awakening. The dark side has a way of enveloping it's prey slowly like a fog moving over the area, making it more difficult to return to the light side, after each visit to the dark side. Many terrible dragons, ogres and multi-headed beast inhabit the dark side and it does not take long for them to invade one's mind, scaring the living daylights out of the poor soul. Any inebriation along with drug indulgence would make this journey that much more exciting but the retreat becomes much more draining, and traumatic and leaves the individual feeling very fatigued.

One dose of a drug will affect two people quite differently, depending on their weight, gender as well as other factors. When given a drug you only have the word of the supplier as to what it is. However this is probably not true. So you are dicing with death, when you partake of a drug that is freely handed out. If you have any medical condition that you are unaware of, this could be fatal. Believing you can hold the supplier responsible, if things go wrong, is a pipe dream. If the drug affects you badly you could end up experiencing serious trauma resulting in fragmented sleep. During which you imagine you are being chased by evil spirits and demons of the underworld. At best you might wake up with a raging thirst and a monumental headache. Next time you might not be so lucky. Playing Russian Roulette with drugs is not smart. The individual who comes over to you and says try this, attempting to place a tablet in the palm of your hand should be avoided at all cost. If saddled with a tablet one should dispose of it immediately. Taking tablets to reach a high is the act of an immature individual, not willing to face life. Think of all your loved ones who could be affected by this simple act of irresponsibility. Why throw your life away, before you have had time to experience it.

The only way back is by breaking off all contact, with those who have delivered you into this predicament. However that alone is not suffice, counselling is imperative and strong companionship to help overcome the terrible urge to descend into the dark again. It can be very arduous, for the counsellors and companions, which can take weeks sometimes even longer. The urge to go back to the dark side is very strong, and promises excitement, it does not relinquish it's prey easily. Others have already ventured too far, they are now inhabited by these despicable monsters, their lives are all but lost. Now they inhabit this DARKNESS and continue to feed it with any available stimulant to avoid having to come down from their high. They will not return to the light side, being possessed by the demons of the underworld, constantly looking to drag souls down deeper into the abyss. Their cries of hopelessness and despair can be heard, by those who are trying to save their poor souls. Hopefully we will never encounter these demons in our lives and the powers of goodness will prevail over them.

Unfortunately the situation is not quite that simple. There is no defining line between the light and the darkness, it is a grey area. The young in particular are constantly wishing to experience real kicks and real excitement, rather than enjoy the beauty of nature around them. For these kicks they must venture into the unknown and often this unknown can be on the dark side. Once, experienced, the urge is always there to return to the same place, or further, for a greater high. That is where the danger lies. Inexperienced souls wishing to up the ante with these kicks, are unknowingly digging a pit for themselves which they just might not be able to crawl out of. If a crime is committed while enjoying a high, this will only make it more difficult to retrace ones steps to the light side. Do this a few times and one begins to think, "oh what the hell-- I'm okay,"----but are you? You are definitely on the slippery slide to the underworld. This can lead to the downfall of many souls as they repeatedly cross over to the dark side for their kicks until they no longer have the inner strength to fight back and regain the light side.

One person much more on the dark side than on the light side now, was Spider Kelly. He stood 188 cm tall, was thin and appeared to be all arms and legs. He enjoyed a zoll of marijuana first thing in the mornings to enable him to focus and start the day in a semi-conscious state. It is highly debatable whether Spider was ever completely sober, as in the course of the day he would partake of whatever stimulants were available. Being employed was not Spider's way, he was in the business of supply and demand, and he kept himself available in case there was a call for a persuader, to encourage someone to alter their way of seeing things.

Spider was extremely dangerous to those he had a supposed grudge against. In spite of his appearance of being reserved and quiet he could, in an instant transform into a fist wielding savage, ready to put the boot in if or when his adversary fell. He had the habit of never looking anyone in the eye. This in itself, should be a warning to anyone encountering Spider, to head for the nearest exit. Once Spider was enraged, and attacked his perceived enemy the only way to stop the onslaught was for three or more, to drag him off his prey, and restrain him until he calmed down. Others would have to provide whatever aid the poor victim needed. Most victims, even those seriously injured, were too afraid to lay charges against Spider for fear of antagonising him into further violence. Spider Kelly was a freelance DESTROYER.

The generous use of the product he was pushing in addition to alcohol, were having a very detrimental effect on Spider's cognitive powers. This resulted in him seeing, danger where there was none. Runners talking to one another now appeared as a conspiracy with the result that he would lash out at anyone he thought was conspiring against him. He was a perfect example of what marijuana could do to someone, and this is one of the "milder" drugs available. It seriously impaired his ability to reason logically. He liked and enjoyed what the marijuana did for him. He was now using it three or four times a day, along with alcohol. So he lived in a state of heightened emotion,with mood swings causing grave concern for those dealing with him on a daily basis. Spider had become unhinged.

EIGHT

The police in Emerald knew Spider, as he had enjoyed the pleasure of their accommodation on many occasions, having been caught trading drugs. Sometimes the stay was overnight for a minor offence, many times longer. Spider had a police record as long as your forearm. Spider's modus operandi was, use everybody to your benefit, and give nothing.

Danny Bell, had come up to the region with three of his friends to have a break. He happened to be sitting in his car using his mobile trying to contact his friends. So they could return to the southern suburbs to their work. Spider seeing Danny in the car wasted no time jumping into the passenger seat, and telling Danny to drive. Now Danny had heard about Spider, and his methods and was confused, saying he was not available as he needed to return to the big city to do his work. Spider repeated his demand "DRIVE". Danny not wishing to be assaulted, and then having to drive Spider, obliged very reluctantly, wondering how he would get out of this terrible mess. Danny a simple fellow from down south, was very upset by this turn of events. If he was forced to drive Spider it would only be, until he could make his escape. Danny disliked drugs, he would never use them, because his mum had warned him about drugs and alcohol.

Danny soon realised that he was driving Spider around to provide drugs, that would then be distributed by his runners. This situation made Danny very unhappy but Spider kept him close, so he could not make a run for it. So Danny did the best he could, he told Spider he needed a certain amount of money for petrol and money for food. The place he was staying at, was for demolition so he needed accommodation. Spider agreed to give him money for petrol and food but said he could come and sleep where Spider was sleeping. At this time Spider was boarding with Mrs. Mathews so Spider said he could come and share the room with him. Danny realised he was between a rock and a hard place, and would have to bide his time. Spider used to get Danny to take him to "George's Pub" where Spider would order a beer, for himself and a coke for Danny. They moved to the snooker room where they would wait for some business to come along. Spider did not sell any narcotics on the premises as George would break his neck, but he did pick up messages telling him where to go to do business. The pub suited Spider as he was from the north side. They used to hang out at "George's Pub" when they were not banned from it. For Spider's unruly behaviour and foul language, which happened every few months. The truth of the matter was, George's patience was wearing very thin, and the next time he caused trouble would be the final straw.

George had a brother, Doug, who was in charge of the waste disposal of Emerald. The depot site was an eight hectare lot situated in the wooded area, 10 kilometres out of town on the north side out of sight. Here the trucks were serviced, cleaned and garaged. The actual tip site was a further 20 kilometres out of town. To collect the refuse in Tegwans' Nest the trucks had to travel a good 60 kilometres one way. Down the east coast and around the bottom of the lake and up to the north west of the lake to Tegwans' Nest. This was the only access by road. It was accessible by boat but that took much longer having to negotiate the oyster farms at four kilometres an hour. This helped to make the residents feel free from authority, and able to do the things they wanted to do. There was no restriction on running ducks, chooks, geese, cows, and horses which gave the place a lovely farm like atmosphere. This was an idyllic place with the forested hills on the west, and the lake on the east, it was a beautiful place to live, in the forest, away from the hustle and bustle of town. Down near the boat ramp was a small community of 40 odd houses, as well as a store that provided milk, bread and other necessities including fuel. The people living here were a mix of retired folk wanting to enjoy a quiet retirement with a few chickens or ducks and enjoy nature. Of the younger couples,some had jobs in town, others were self employed and had big gear that was easier to accommodate on a bigger property.

Here at Tegwans' Nest, those who wanted to be free and enjoy nature, took up residence on land ranging from 10 acres to 40 -50 acre lots, pursuing their dreams. Some plots of land had residences on them, others required the owner to build accommodation. Life in the valley below the ranges was good. It did not take long, before some enterprising individual, decided to see about taking steps to satisfy his desire, for some additional stimulation. Soon others followed suit. Growing the weed in the small clearings in the forest became a common practice, both for home consumption, and for local sale. Should the forces ever find the weed it was not on anybody's land so no charges could be levied without evidence, of criminality against someone. Because of the distance from Emerald to Tegwans' Nest it was possible to get an early warning of an impending visit from the powers that be. Usually Terry Hegarty a local senior constable in the police would let a contact in Tegwans' Nest know. For this service Terry received enough weed for his personal use. Terry who enjoyed a zoll and believed it to be harmless, did not see his way clear to reporting it's use, in moderation, to the higher ups.

However the big problem with the weed was "moderation", there was always the urge to produce more. Some of the locals could not contain themselves, soon the forests around there were studded with little patches of young marijuana plants and this resulted in a jump in the weed for sale. One of the residents, Jimmy, who knew Doug, the manager of the rubbish collection. He had done repairs to the hydraulic cylinders on the trucks. Asked Doug if there was any way they could send the weed they could not sell locally to the big city for sale. Doug was very interested in this idea. After some thought he reckoned he could increase the size of the lockers on the sides of the trucks to accommodate the precious cargo. However to get it to the big city was another question. Then he remembered there was a Dutchman who ran a cleaning business in the city and he had a property on the shores of the lake. Anton de Grootte used to travel in a commercial van, to the city every Monday or Tuesday with cleaning products for his staff. It was not that full that they could not conceal some weed in it. What was even better was that Anton had a yacht which he kept berthed at his private jetty on the lake, or at one of the berths on the south side of the bridge near the entrance to the lake. He used the yacht to go to the city when going by vehicle was unwise.

****

One day some of the local characters, having just smoked a fair bit of weed, decided to see if they could knock some of the residential post boxes out of the ground. (The boxes were each placed on a post and planted in the earth near the gates, of the various properties, along the roadside). This was done with one fellow, Karl, kneeing in the back of the ute with a chunk of 50mm x50mm pine wood while his mates sat up front driving the ute. Initially this was done at a slow speed but Karl urged them to drive more quickly, and so they did. Karl took a huge swing at the next post box and a tremendous shock raced up his arms, into his shoulders and back paralysing him and the next thing Karl knew, he was lying in the dirt. The pole for the post box had been concreted in the ground. For the next couple of weeks Karl was very sore, with many bruises and not in the mood for jokes about post boxes.

****

Oliver one of the local growers, decided he was not happy growing small amounts of cannabis. He wanted to do some serious production, and he would do it on his own. He did not see his way clear, to go in with the others sending extra weed to the city by way of Doug's pick-up service. Believing he could do better by selling it himself. So he bought a quantity of big plastic pots, filled them with potting mix, then planted small marijuana plants in them. These he tended judiciously until the crop was ready, moving them under cover when he heard police choppers overhead. Then he and his partner would package the crop and Oliver would head for the big city, at night. This seemed to work and Oliver would arrive back home, after a few days wearing new clothes. After a number of years the police in unmarked cars paid Oliver a visit and, "low and behold" there were 48 pots with beautiful marijuana plants thriving in them. In the house they found more weed packaged, ready for sale. Oliver was unable to explain, in a satisfactory manner, how this situation came about.

He was taken into custody to Emerald, charged, and given bail until his court appearance. A couple of weeks later Oliver was sent down for 14 months. The story told around the area was that Oliver had signed on as a member of the crew, on a fishing trawler, and would be back once his contract was finished. However his partner, who had been away from the property on the occasion of the police visit, did not suffer the same fate, and was open about the fact that Oliver was inside. Oliver reappeared a free man with a nose that had been broken and some scars on his body, having completed his fourteen months stint in jail. He seemed to lack the tanned body one would expect from a crew member on a trawler. Now he had a dilemma, he needed an income, apart from his unemployment benefits. His partner was asking for a refund of the mortgage payments she had made on his behalf, while he was residing at Her Majesty's Pleasure. Not one to engage in hard work if there was an alternative option, he eventually decided he would just grow a little weed to help him out until something better turned up.

****

One afternoon there was a serious alert, there was a fire raging over the ranges on the west side and it had jumped the river and was headed for Tegwans' Nest. Everybody was told to be on a five minute evacuation order as the fire got closer. The choppers could be seen coming over the crest of the hills on the west side. To fly down to the lake to fill the big buckets, suspended beneath them, with water to return to fight the fire. This situation lasted a good hour with the residents very apprehensive, until the firefighters finally got the upper hand and the locals were told the fire was under control. It was a really close call for the residents and some were quite traumatised as they would have had to leave animals behind, to try and escape from a raging fire. This was a very sobering thought and residents tried clearing areas around their homes and outbuildings to minimise their chances of having to evacuate in the future. Some did not realise a raging fire, is extremely ferocious, hot, loud and races at speed, destroying everything in it's path. It jumps roadways and sports fields, while the embers are thrown out in all directions ensuring that the fire continues to spread in all directions. It is absolutely terrifying to those who come in contact with it. Nothing can stop it, but water and plenty of it.

****

The other serious disadvantage to living at Tegwans' nest, was that an ambulance took a long time to get here. This is what happened to two of the nature lovers. Vail and Beth had come up from a city to the south to find some peace and quiet. They built a house on their property and were enjoying the good life when Vail had a heart attack and his wife Beth, phoned immediately for an ambulance. The medics arrived just in time, and administered first aid keeping Vail alive. Then they had to travel back to Emerald and a further 30 kilometres to the hospital in the next town of Eden. Vail survived the ride to spend nearly two weeks in hospital while the doctors and nurses slowly patched him up. This gave Vail something to think about, it had been touch and go whether he would make it. The fact that the medics, in the ambulance, were so proficient at their task, must surely have made a big difference to his chances of staying alive. Twelve days later Vail standing with his walking stick in hand, was discharged from the hospital, thanking all the staff for their great work. Beth and Vail discussed their situation, and decided they would not tempt fate a second time. So they sold their property, and moved into Emerald, where they bought a house that was close to the amenities. Vail's abilities were compromised so it was the wisest idea to relocate. The club was a short walk down the road where they could enjoy a drink and a meal and relax a while. The supermarket was just a little further and the hardware store was next to the supermarket. This sure made things a lot easier, while the ambulance station was just around the corner.

****

Vail had never taken drugs he disliked the thought of it. He had a friend Peter who was a good fellow, who would go out of his way to help another. However Peter had been introduced to cigarettes, drink and the weed in his early teens and had used them fairly regularly ever since. Over the years Vail had seen how the drink and drugs had gained control of him. How he managed to turn up at work every day was a miracle. But he did, and this probably in some way, helped to slow Peter's downward spiral, unable to rid himself of this curse. After repeated stints in rehab, Peter was sent into care, as he was in danger of hurting himself when suffering an hallucination attack, which now occurred quite frequently. Sadly, he died at age 42 after being unable to wean himself of the drink and drugs. Alcohol and drugs are a deadly combination causing a person to exit in a state of grandiose contentment, removed from reality.

NINE

There was a fellow, Thomas, who lived out at Tegwans' Nest, with his wife and two children. They had a property and were trying to get money together to build a house. Thomas had a natural gift, he could paint landscapes. So he painted, and as he painted he improved so his paintings were sold for better prices, at the markets. Later he was commissioned by a well to do property owner to do a large landscape. This proved to be very successful, and other orders were placed for his services. His work became very popular, and financially rewarding until he was able to make enough money to build a lovely house for his family.

One afternoon at work Terry Hegarty overheard the Sergeant saying they would be doing a drug inspection of the rubbish truck, doing the Tegwans' Nest run the next day after it had finished its pick ups. Terry needed to get word to Doug to give them time to blow out the lockers on the truck with compressed air before the morning run. Terry went into the toilet cubicle when nobody else was in the toilet and put through a call to Doug at the depot. Warning him of the inspection on the Tegwans' Nest truck the following day. After finishing his shift that afternoon he phoned his contact in Tegwans' Nest. Giving them notice, not to load any weed on the truck the following morning. So the inspection next morning gave the rubbish truck a clean bill of health.

On her first day at "Keane and Associates" Natalie was met by Gerry who welcomed her to the firm, saying that if there were any things she did not know or understand it was essential that she asked either her fellow workers or him. Before being shown to her place of work Natalie explained how she had recorded a conversation Rodney had with an Estelle Brown, who had come to him for legal aid. She produced the tape and handed it to Gerry, who said he would deal with it.

Gerry listened to the tape, and was disgusted with Rodney's behaviour trying to take advantage of a lady in distress. He took the tape down to the police station and handed it in to Sergeant Lewis explaining the circumstances under which it was taped, and the two individuals involved. Rodney Pleasant was well known to the local police as there had been complaints about his behaviour over a number of years. Sergeant Lewis reviewed the tape with a detective from the vice squad, Det. Sgt. Bert Lowe. The detective said he would make further enquiries, and the tape was placed into evidence. Unfortunately, so far Rodney had not broken the law, it was a matter of time.

Shirley had a good friend, named Eli Young whom she had known since junior school. They met on the first day of school and had been best friends ever since. Eli came from a disadvantaged background, her father had never been able to hold down a job for long so finances were always very tight. Her mother had a cleaning business which required her working at nights. She had built the business up over the years and this was what kept things going. Early on in their junior years the girls would go to Shirley's home after school, where her mum would give them some lunch and then they would settle down and do their homework together. Later on in the afternoon Shirley would walk halfway home with Eli. As the girls turned 15 they were looking for ways to earn some money in the afternoons. The two went to a coffee and sandwich bar to see if Eli might obtain some afternoon employment. Lucky for Eli the manager said "yes her services could come in very handy." Eli was asked to start the next day as they had been contemplating recruiting a new worker. So Eli worked every afternoon after school and on Saturday morning. Eli was a quick learner and she soon knew what was required of her and the manager was impressed with her attitude to the work. While Eli worked at her job, Shirley helped her father in the clothing and sportswear store and earned some money. The money earned from these jobs, the girls used to pay for their Taekwondo Martial Arts Classes. Eli's mum was proud of her daughter getting a job and trying to improve her lot.

In her early life, Eli had virtually no input, from a person of the opposite sex, as her father was very seldom at home. When he was he had nothing to say to her. Her mum did her best to raise the girls, but she worked nights cleaning offices and units. By far the biggest influence came from Shirley and her parents. Fortunately, Shirley came from a good cohesive, loving and caring family, so what Shirley passed on to Eli, was sound advice that Shirley had been told to do. In this way Eli learned how to behave, and most of what she knew about the other sex. Don, Shirley's father always treated her just the same as Shirley, knowing she had limited contact with her father. Unfortunately most of the boys Eli knew, from school did nothing to inspire her to have contact with them, so she ignored them. There was just no real male lead in her life. Shirley was her leader, when the two of them decided to enrol in martial arts.

Of the little money left she gave her mother half. Slowly as they grew older she noticed how Shirley treated different males in a different manner. She followed suite believing this was the thing to do. However there was always a wall, between her and the opposite sex as she did not see most of them as particularly interesting. So the two girls grew up learning Taekwondo once a week in the evening. By the time the girls finished school Eli had worked herself into a full time position at the coffee bar, and second in line to the boss for time served in the business. She knew all about the ordering of the bread and buns, the morning roster for coffee to be delivered to various businesses. All the standing orders that needed preparing each morning, and what time they needed to be delivered.

In fact when Rosie (the boss) was out of the shop Eli was really running the show. After leaving school Shirley went into her father clothing and sportswear shop to work and in time became manager as her father was getting on in years. Eli worked in the coffee bar for a further six years until Rosie had decided she wanted out. Eli seizing her opportunity suggested she take it over. Rosie said by all means if she could raise the money. Eli sprang into action contacting Shirley and asking her what to do. Shirley got hold of Tom who phoned Gerry with the idea. Gerry asked some questions and said he would try to contact Chap, a financier who had strong links to Emerald to see if he could help with some finance. The following afternoon Gerry got back to Tom saying Chap was willing to help in this case, as it met the criterion of a very deserving situation. Eli was very grateful to all concerned saying she would not let them down. Eli operated the little shop very successfully like that for a further 18 months.

Although the premises did not look big, it was very surprising what they produced in a single day. The shop was located in an arcade, between Head Street and Head Lane. The tremendous increase in business during holiday times, allowed Eli to negotiate a deal on the premises next to her present locality as it was twice the size and she really needed the space. She believed that maintaining a position in the arcade was best for two reasons. Firstly the business had been in the arcade for many years now, and to move it might lead the clientele to think that she had closed the shop. Secondly being in the arcade meant that the area was locked at night providing security. The shop became known as "The Coffee and Sandwich Bar". The extra space also allowed her to place a couple of tables and chairs out for customers wishing to sit and enjoy their purchase.

In the off seasons Eli and Shirley usually had lunch together, either down near the northern reaches of the lake under the beautiful fig trees that provided shade for so many, or on the terrace in the winter sun, feeding the seagulls with snippets of bread or chips. Eli was not married which was probably from seeing, how her mum had battled with her father who provided so little to the household. It had created a very strained relationship between her parents which left her feeling very uneasy. This was not a topic that Eli cared to talk about, even to Shirley, as it hurt. Both her parents had since passed away and she only had one younger sister who was married but they were not close.

Eli and Shirley were as close as any two sisters could be, and Shirley hoped that Eli would meet her soul mate. They talked to each other every day usually more than once. The two businesses were only 200 metres apart and Shirley started her working day, with a mug of cappuccino from Eli's Coffee Bar. Shirley would have liked to encourage Eli to go out with more men, but she could feel that any pushing from her could result in forcing them apart. This Shirley was very careful to avoid. Eli was a brunette with beautiful blue eyes, a delightful sense of humour and stood 176 cm tall. There had been some suitors over the years, but Eli was just not prepared to make a commitment. She had a golden Labrador that she showered with affection knowing that it would be reciprocated.

Eli lived in an old house in Short street, in the older part of town. It was small but well fenced and the owner had been a friend of her mum, while she was alive. Because of that, Eli paid a nominal rental. The first real contact Eli had with a male outside of her little coffee shop was Tom Edwards, until that stage she had really considered them a non event. Often on the weekends Eli would spend time with Shirley and Tom on the boat or enjoying a barbecue at their home. Tom was fond of Eli and tried to include her, where possible, in their activities so she would not be alone and become depressed. Eli learned to know and trust Tom, and he would joke with her. Gerry and Bev also got on with her, and Eli and Bev would often be seen discussing different styles of clothing. Bev would say much depended on the lady's height, shape and colour. Working with those three things she could make a lady look very attractive.

One Wednesday morning Shirley was on the north side of town, dropping off some papers at "Keane and Associates" for Gerry to peruse. Tom was considering investing in a small block of flats, coming on the market shortly. As she made her way back to her car, Rodney came along. When passing her, he tried to grab her hand and pull her towards him. Shirley was too quick for him and slapped his hand away and said "get lost you pathetic weasel". He became enraged at this and shouted abuse back at Shirley but she had wasted no time in disappearing from sight. Shirley was not upset by Rodney's behaviour as she had seen in the past, that he would make a pass at other women. However she did not want to be associated with him, as she disliked him.

****

Meanwhile back in Tegwans' Nest there had been a bit of action. One weekday morning a warning came through that the police, would be making a marijuana raid out there in the afternoon. Apparently there had been a influx of weed in Emerald and Sergeant Fred Lewis was not happy. All the growers had to ensure there were no boot prints in the soil around the plants in the forest. So one of them cut a green branch with plenty of foliage and walked around the area where the plants were, dragging the branch behind him to destroy any evidence of footprints. Furthermore, all tools and other identifiable equipment had to disappear. By lunch everything was clean, and neat so it was now in the lap of the Gods.

After 2 pm. two people movers filled with police arrived and everybody expressed their surprise when ten constables emerged from the vehicles. They were there to see how the residents had been behaving. They entered the forest area and after some time returned with a small quantity of cannabis plants. Sergeant Fred Lewis was surprised that the number of plants were so few. He was under the impression that they would find a substantial haul of cannabis plants. So after two hours of searching they departed. The reason there were so few marijuana plants was that some of the fellows had pulled as many small plants as they could out of the soil, and discarded them to avoid a major incident. The truth must never be revealed. The guys could always plant more, the loss was allowed for in a business where you always had to be on the alert for big brother. They survived, and started planting more cannabis in the following days.

TEN

Late one afternoon an elderly couple, Ted and Mavis Butler, living in Wharf Street, not far from the fisherman's co-op, heard a car screeching away and came out to see what the noise was about. All Ted saw was a white convertible car parked near the co-op and what seemed to be someone slouched behind the wheel. Ted walked over to the car wondering if he might help and got the fright of his life, seeing a lady slumped over the steering wheel with her door open. Her right foot was still on the gravel and blood seeping through her blouse. Ted was very upset by this scene, and hurried home telling his wife, to phone for the ambulance. Ted told his wife, Mavis she should not go out there as it was very distressing. At about 5.05 pm a call came through on the emergency channel, that an incident had occurred and an ambulance, a doctor, and the police were required urgently down at the fisherman's co- op to render assistance. The Butlers stood on their front porch watching the events unfold across the way. From this distance it was okay, as one could not see any detail of what was actually happening. The thought was very distressing for Mavis, so Ted took his wife back into the house.

The ambulance crew on arrival, found a lady slumped over the steering wheel of her car and she was deceased. Sergeant Lewis was the first policeman on the site and on closer examination recognised the deceased as Shirley Edwards. The police doctor was in attendance and declared the lady deceased. As the murder squad and forensics would be some time arriving, it was decided to move the deceased to the mortuary right away. Sergeant Lewis, notified base that the deceased was Shirley Edwards. He was told to immediately contact, Tom Edwards and speak to him at the station, explaining what had happened, before he heard it from a third person. Sergeant Lewis contacted Tom Edwards by mobile and asked him to come down to the police station immediately. This Tom did and he was ushered into one of the interview rooms and asked to take a seat. Then Sergeant Lewis broke the sad news to Tom. He just sat there, in shock, his brain refusing to accept what he was being told. How could this be?

He was trying to comprehend what Sergeant Lewis was telling him and it was not coming through. It was not easy to absorb what he was being told, he appeared to have a mental block, saving him from a complete shutdown. Tom then asked Sgt. Lewis if he was sure that it was Shirley. Sgt. Lewis replied in the affirmative and Tom just collapsed. Sgt. Lewis got him some water and after some time, Tom pulled himself up and asked what had happened. To Tom everything was happening in slow motion, almost as if he was out of his body floating as an observer. The voices of the speakers seemed to come from a great distance away. Sgt. Lewis explained that Shirley had come out of the Fisherman's Co op with fish and chips, and went to her car, and there seemed to have been a confrontation of some sort, and as she tried to drive away she had been shot twice. Tom was in total disbelief and asked to be taken to the site. Sergeant Lewis obliged, and at the scene the area was cordoned off with police tape with Shirley's car in the middle. She had already been transported to the mortuary, due to the fact the forensics team would be some time getting there. It was thought to be unwise to leave the deceased "in situ" in the heat, with many people in the vicinity looking on.

Tom just stood and stared at the sight, he was

finding it very difficult to process the information. Fish and chips strewn around the driver's side of the vehicle. He was not allowed inside the police tape. Tom's mind was in a state of turmoil and disbelief how could this be happening to him. He asked Sgt. Lewis to take him to the mortuary, which he did. Tom, first phoned Gerry and Eli to tell them the terrible news, and he burst into tears, talking to Eli on the phone. They both said they would come immediately. When Gerry and Eli arrived Tom hugged Gerry, and then embraced Eli. They burst into tears, holding one another tightly for some time. Arrangements were being made for them to identify the deceased as Shirley Edwards. After a while they went to the viewing room to see Shirley and confirm her identity. They all felt very traumatised by this, and stumbled back into the passage. Tom then phoned Don to tell him the very sad news, and he was very upset, and wanted to come down to the mortuary. Tom managed to dissuade him, as he was sure it would be too much for him to see Shirley like that. When they left the mortuary the three of them went around to see Don, and express their deep sympathy at his loss. They each gave Don a big hug, and after sitting for a while making small talk, Don said he would like to be alone, so the three left.

Back at the mortuary again to collect Eli's car. Gerry was very distressed and gave Tom and Eli each a hug and said he needed to go home, so Eli and Tom went to pick his car up from the police station and they went to Tom's house. They were both extremely traumatised by this horrific murder and did not wish to be alone. They felt as if they were "on set" in a slow motion horror movie, everything they absorbed was in slow motion. Eli could not stop crying feeling very alone without Shirley so she did all she could do, just cling to Tom. Eventually Tom said they had better try and eat something so he made two omelettes, but all they seemed to do was move the food around the plates as they were talking. Tom said he did not wish Eli to be alone, so they drove down to her house and packed some clothes and toiletries, and returned to Tom's house along with her trusty golden Labrador, Honey, who was just happy to be with Eli. They eventually went to bed and Tom awoke in the night to hear Eli sobbing so he went to her room and got into bed with her and held her close. They must have fallen asleep like that, as next morning they awoke in the same position.

It was obvious to Tom that Eli was in no condition to go to work. Tom phoned in telling them, that

Eli would not be in for the next week. Tom did not feel able to return to work so he phoned Craig, his chargehand, and told him he would be working from home for the next few days. Tom took Eli down to see a doctor, who prescribed some sleeping pills and anti-depressants for both of them. Telling them they would need to take them as prescribed every day for the next week. There were no repeats, so if they needed more Tom should bring her back. There were a number of jobs, in the workshop, at home that could keep him busy for a while. However it was so difficult to concentrate on the job at hand that Tom realised he needed to do something else. Tom took Eli in his arms and held her close until she stopped crying. He then said they should take Honey onto the front lawn and play with her. This they did and it helped to stop Eli crying for a while. The healing process is slow and cannot be rushed. So Tom and Eli spent time in the garden walking around and talking about the different plants. After a while they felt a bit more settled. Tom realised the only way he could look after Eli was to arrange things so that she was physically helping him do whatever it was that needed doing. This worked as Eli was obliged to concentrate on performing the small tasks Tom requested of her. Although they were in the same situation Tom felt he needed to take the lead and try to get some sanity back in their lives. The hurt was unbearable but Tom knew he could not let it overcome them. Eli was obviously not coping very well and was crying most of the time. She needed constant care, so he made sure she was with him all the time. They did not do much work but it did help them settle a little. Unfortunately this situation continued for the week and they had to return to the doctor for more medication. Eli was still unable to focus on anything for very long. Eli was still in a bad way and Tom felt very shaky.

So Tom felt he could not, return to work and leave Eli, alone. He phoned Craig asking if things were okay and said if they needed him he would be at home. Eli needed Tom around, as alone she just collapsed. Tom advised Eli's business she would not be back that week. Tom just did jobs around the house, and in his workshop making sure, Eli was there with him all the time. Losing a loved one who is elderly is a shock, but not completely unexpected. However losing a loved one, in the prime of their life, is absolutely devastating. The realisation that your loved one will not be returning, takes weeks to filter through. Every so often it hits you again and you feel your knees giving way. Unfortunately this process continues for a very long time and one will never get over it. Returning to work is probably the best way to aid recovery. After the second week, Tom realised both he, and Eli had to try to return to work, if they were ever going to make any serious effort, to normalise. Tom spoke to Eli gently telling her they both needed to make an effort to get back to work. However he would take her, and fetch her while she was still taking the drugs. If she needed him he would be a phone call away. Eli understood she needed to try and straighten herself out. They had been back to the doctor for repeat scripts for Eli.

The gaping hole created by the loss of a loved one, very slowly gets smaller over time but it never disappears. One has to get used to living with the hurt. Any tiny incident, may cause the grief to return, like a flood trying to engulf one. The following Monday, Tom took Eli to work and proceeded to Edward Security taking time to see that Craig had everything under control. Craig was a disciplined man and it showed in his work, Tom was very glad he had been able to employ him. He never panicked and could analyse a situation very quickly. Craig was well rewarded by Tom, showing him, Tom valued his services. They had a good relationship and Craig knew Tom was available to discuss anything that might be worrying him. Once he was happy about things under Craig's supervision he went up into his office to look at some quotes he needed to finalise, for three companies erecting large warehouses in the industrial area.

Gerry phoned to hear how things were going, and Tom explained that the police knew nothing more at this time, Gerry said he would come around after work. Tom went down to the police station with Eli in the afternoon desperate for news. However Sergeant Lewis said nothing further had come to light, and they were waiting on the results from the lab on the shell casings. He said the police were as baffled as Tom, as nothing about the shooting made any sense. Tom phoned Gerry to say he and Eli were going down to One Mile beach, and would Gerry and Bev please join them. He and Eli then made their way down to One Mile beach where Shirley, Eli, Tom, Bev and Gerry often swam, and they sat on the sand talking about the good times they had experienced at this venue. After a while Eli asked Tom if he would take her to the site of Shirley's dreadful murder, but Tom was very reluctant to do that. He said maybe later on when things were better he would, but right know it would be too distressing for her. Eli reasoned he was probably right so she did not push the issue.

Later, when it was getting dark Gerry and Bev went home but they were both very shaken by this horrendous event. Tom and Eli went down to the take away, got something to eat and went back to Tom's house. Eli asked if it was okay for her to stay for a few more days, as she felt very fragile Tom said she could stay, as long as she liked as he believed she would be safer where he could protect her. They had a discussion about how they felt and what to do. They decided to continue going to work so as to keep occupied, trying to stop themselves thinking, about Shirley's demise, all the time. Eli thought how lucky she was that she knew Tom so well, otherwise she would have been in limbo. Tom said he would phone Eli during the day to see how she was doing, and Eli felt reassured by that. Really she felt absolutely terrified at the thought of being alone, at this time, and she knew Tom would never take advantage of her.

ELEVEN

The local police realised this was murder, so the forensic team as well as the murder squad, were called in. The specialist murder squad came from the big city, and only arrived late that night. Meanwhile the area had been fenced off with police tape and a constable was posted to protect the site. The forensic team which came up from Arncliffe were there by 8 pm, and immediately started processing the car and the area all around it. They had lights up and they would be busy until who knows when. There was no disputing the fact that this was murder, however the forensic team was facing some major problems. The fish and chips were all over the interior of the convertible, and out onto the gravel. There were shoe markings in the gravel to show some sort of a altercation had taken place, but no discernible shoe patterns of evidentiary value. The other car was not seen by anyone, and there was very little contact between Shirley, and her assailant. They would process Shirley's blouse around the right upper arm, and shoulder where she had apparently been grabbed, and her left foot which was very swollen now. Hopefully there might be something to work with. The two shells could potentially have a story to tell. Apart from that there seemed to be very little to go on. However the team would do everything they could to find the cowardly assassin. One of the forensic team was sent to the morgue to examine Shirley's body for any evidence. As nobody had seen a vehicle drive away, from the scene, the constables would be doing door to door knocks, hoping to find a witness.

The homicide squad was contacted and Det. Sgt. Adam Poole and Det. Inspector Barry Wallis were despatched from the big city to take over the case. They arrived at 11pm and were given an account of what the local police, thought happened, before proceeding to the crime scene. They took some time to just view the whole area, and then proceeded to approach the site of the crime, where Shirley's car was, and it was possible to get an idea of where Shirley and her assailant had been due to scruff marks, in the powdery road base close to the driver's side of Shirley's car. They did their best to re-enact the event, and came to the conclusion that the assailant must have had contact with Shirley prior to shooting her, otherwise the fish and chips would have been confined to the vehicle. So it was reasoned that the aggressor had possibly pulled at her right arm to gain her attention, and she had retaliated. How? Her hands were full ! She was holding a parcel of fish and chips as well as her handbag. How could she have responded? It was at this stage that Det. Sgt. Poole asked who knew Shirley well. They referred him to Gerry Keane, as they did not want to cause any extra trauma for Tom by contacting him. However due to the lateness of the hour they waited till morning to contact him.

In the morning when Gerry was contacted he told Det. Sgt. Poole that Shirley was a competent exponent of the art of Taekwondo, a Korean Martial Arts discipline. It was concluded that the assailant had parked behind Shirley's car to approach her from behind. So this seemed to suggest that Shirley had swung around when the attacker pulled on her right arm, and she dispatched a vicious kick with her left foot at the assailant's groin. This seemed to make sense as, if the attacker had wished to kill her he would not have bothered to touch her, he would simply have shot her in the car. However the assailant must have swayed or moved slightly to avoid the kick. Otherwise he would have been in no condition to continue the attack. So the shooting was as a result of her retaliation. The attacker became angry at her resistance to his assault. From the evidence it seemed clear, that the attacker was not aware Shirley was a martial arts expert, or he would have been more careful. The attacker had come to teach her a lesson, not to kill her but her reaction resulted in him losing his temper and shooting her. The assailant had a short fuse.

Det. Sgt. Poole interviewed Mavis, and Ted Butler about the event and what they heard. Ted said he had heard the squeal of tyres on the road, and had gone outside to see what was on the go. However there were no cars in sight except for the White BMW parked near the fisherman's co-op. He had gone over to see if the person needed help, and saw blood on the lady's blouse and fish and chips spread all over, so he called to his wife to get the ambulance. Ted Butler said, when questions, that he had not heard a gun fired, only the sound of the tyres on the road. So far the police had no leads except for two spent 9mm cartridges, and that was all. Ballistics would try to match them to any records they might have, but that would take some time. After two days the pathology report was released, and it said that Shirley had suffered two gunshot wounds, one to the back of her right shoulder, and one to the base of her skull, and this was the fatal shot. Both shots had been fired about two metres from Shirley as there was minimal gunshot residue on her clothing. Shirley was sober and had no drugs in her system. She had bruising to her upper right arm, as well as severe bruising to the her left foot, with the first and second metatarsal bones fractured as if she had kicked something really hard, but no further injuries. Nothing to help explain how, and why this horrendous crime was committed. Tom was informed he was now able to arrange for Shirley's cremation.

Tom could not face, going down to the undertakers to arrange for Shirley's funeral, so he asked Gerry if he would. Gerry obliged, and went down to the funeral parlour, explaining what Tom wanted, and that it was to be a cremation. They assured Gerry, Tom's wishes would be met, all would be taken care of, and they would pick up Tom, Eli and Don, at Tom's house, on the day, in time for the service. There must have been well over two hundred mourners at the crematorium, friends from the lifesavers and Taekwondo and many friends from her school days. Tom and Eli sat in the front row, along with Don, Gerry, Bev and Jane. Tom was in no condition to say anything so Gerry went up, and spoke of Shirley's life in Emerald, and all the things she had done. She had run a top business in town, providing clothing and sportswear. Shirley had been very involved in promoting Emerald. Going down to the big city every year for two days, to entice visitors up to the beautiful area around Emerald, to enjoy all the pleasures it offered. She had progressed to black belt in the art of Taekwondo and she spent time as a lifesaving instructor helping train the teenage girls in lifesaving.

After the ceremony the casket disappeared through the curtains, and the mourners listened to "Sunshine on my shoulder" by John Denver being played, one of Shirley's favourite songs. The close friends gathered at Tom's home, where Don, Eli and Tom thanked the mourners for coming, and asked them to please have some of the refreshments provided. Eli had insisted that her Coffee Bar and sandwich shop provide the eats, and a very good job they did. Don proposed a toast to Shirley, and suggested that they concentrate on the good qualities Shirley portrayed in her life, and remember her for them. Gerry, Bev and Jane were the last to leave.

Eight days after the homicide Sgt. Lewis phoned Tom, and asked him to come down to the Station, as he had some news. On Tom's arrival they went into an interview room. Sgt. Lewis informed Tom that they had feedback from the lab, and the shell casings matched casings from a murder in the city a month previously. The two bullets removed from Shirley's body, showed firearm markings which indicated it was the same firearm, used in the murder of Shirley as in the assassination of an underworld figure in the city. As she was not engaged in any drug activity, they were considering whether this was a tragic case of mistaken identity, as there was no way Shirley had any connection to the gangs peddling drugs in the city. The shooting in the city was definitely drug related, but there were no major drug dealers in Emerald.

As Gerry's relations with Sgt. Lewis were very different to Tom's, because of the fact he was working with juveniles in trouble. Gerry was privy to some thoughts and ideas that the police were following in this egregious killing. He felt he might make some enquiries of his own with some contacts he had in the city, it could do no harm.

Life went on, but not too well for Tom and Eli, they clung to each other for support. As far as Eli was concerned Tom was all she had, now that Shirley had been taken from her, and Gerry felt helpless as he was unable to give much assistance, although he made himself available as, and when he was needed. Tom realised that Gerry was standing by, and expressed his gratitude for his concern. Tom treated Eli very gently realising how dreadful this despicable act was making Eli feel. They saw the doctor who was agreeable to giving her further prescriptions, for sedatives and sleeping tablets to help over the coming week. Tom and Eli made regular visits to Don to see how he was coping but it was difficult to know as he kept his feelings under very strict check. Tom told Gerry about the information they had gleaned from Sgt. Lewis, with regard to the handgun having been used on a murder in the city one month before Shirley's shooting. Gerry did not believe someone from the city had come to Emerald, to shoot Shirley, he believed there had to be another explanation. Maybe the gun had been passed on to someone in Emerald, however there was nobody in Emerald that wanted Shirley dead, was there?

On hearing of this atrocious deed George wasted no time in phoning Tom and Eli to express the heartfelt sympathy of all his family, in the egregious death of Shirley. In the pub the consensus of opinion seemed to be that it was a mistaken identity, as Shirley was hardly a gangster. She was the lovely lady that ran the sportswear shop in the main street of Emerald. Over the ensuing weeks this unbelievable act of horror was discussed by all and sundry, with nobody providing a plausible explanation for the deed. The people of Emerald felt they needed to do something in her memory. Her actions, particularly in the training of junior lifesavers, had touched many families in the years she had been involved with them. It was decided to have a collection to see if they could raise enough money for a plaque, in her honour somewhere near the lifesavers club. The people of Emerald responded very generously and raised enough money for a bronze plaque. This was attached to the wall at the entrance to the lifesavers club, for all to see.

TWELVE

Meanwhile, being nomadic by nature, Spider chose to move up to Eden for a while with Danny in tow, as the police in Emerald were giving Spider a hard time. In Eden, Spider and Danny were getting settled, as they had no plans to return to Emerald in the short term. Darren, Spider's mate was actually a distant relative to Spider so there was no likelihood of them getting kicked out in a hurry. Spider and Danny were given the room at the back of the house which had it's own exterior, entry door. This suited Spider just fine, they could come and go as they liked. However running the Emerald business was difficult from Eden. Spider explained that at the moment that is what they had to do. They would make two trips a day to Emerald to keep the supply chain operational, once in the morning and once before dark.

They had made some contacts in the local pub

to supply weed, and the pub had a snooker room so they felt reasonably organised. Danny had a side line collecting used air conditioners, stripping them for the copper inside, which he sold to the scrap metal dealer, just out of town, for cash. This all came about as Danny saw some old air cons in the backyard and started disassembling them. Inside he found some copper piping, so he stripped this out of each of the air cons lying around. He asked Darren where the air cons came from. Darren said from a building site not far up the road. So a mini industry was born, Danny would talk Spider into going up to the building site, ostensibly to load air cons into the neighbours trailer but with the idea he sell some weed up there. This worked out well, the neighbour used his trailer very seldom, so he was happy to let them use it. The remains of the air cons, they dumped around a stump in the back yard of Darren's house. Spider was obliged to help loading the air cons and bring them back to Darren's place. This was not a thriving industry but it helped. They had to do something to help pay their rent, as there was no alternative at the moment, this would have to do. The plus being they were meeting people, which could possibly come in handy at a later date, if an alibi was required. Spider was trying to do a bit of trading, but he did not know many people so he needed to be careful.

Det. Insp. Barry Wallis and Det. Sgt. Adam Poole of the murder squad, took a long hard look at Tom and his activities, as he was automatically the number one suspect. Tom's life was an open book, so it was possible for the police to track his every move. As it was necessary for his secretary to get hold of him in case of a serious problem with any of the big business alarms. So the police had one of their easiest jobs. Going through Tom's records for the times concerned they could find not a shred of evidence, that he could possibly have arranged Shirley's death. Gerry had told the police that Tom was incapable of committing murder. Tom's mobile was put through analysis by the lab IT specialists, and they were unable to find any contradiction to his statement. His secretary was interviewed and his daily diary was cross checked against what the secretary had stated, no discrepancies could be found. Everything to do with Tom and his actions over the past months, were proven to be as stated by Tom and his secretary. Tom could not have had anything to do with Shirley's egregious murder. The police continued their interrogation, now Eli was in the firing line. Tom was incensed, how could they possibly imagine that Eli who had grown up with Shirley and had known her for 20 odd years, could ever contemplate such a dastardly deed. The police insisted in looking into where she was at the time and if her mobile could shed any light on the issue, but to no avail. Eli was at work from early each morning, and her mobile showed all the calls she had made during the relevant time period with no hint of any underhand dealings. It was really bizarre to even imagine, that Eli could have had a hand in Shirley's death. The crime was completely baffling and the big city police had no answers to date, either, and pressure was mounting on the force to come up with an answer.

Tom took time one evening to sit Eli down, and explain to her how very much he needed her emotional support, but there were people who would look at their close relationship, and conclude that he and Eli were having an affair, and that led to Tom arranging for Shirley to be shot. He said he did not want to loose Eli, as she meant a tremendous amount to him, and she was helping him over this very distressing time. Eli responded by saying that she was very fond of Tom, and he was helping her just as much as she was helping him. They each knew they needed the other very much. Neither Eli nor Tom had ever been exposed to trauma of this magnitude, it was scary. Holding hands tightly they decided to carry on phoning one another everyday, and Tom would invariably pick up Eli after work each afternoon. Eli was terrified of having to stay at home alone, and Tom could understand her fear, she had just had the major part of her life ripped from her. So she was clinging to Tom for some stability. How could Tom say "you will just have to deal with it" he himself was in the same boat, and feeling equally numb. So Eli stayed at Tom's home, and he took her to and from work each day. They spent most evenings just talking about the events, and trying to fathom how to proceed. Two months after the terrible event Eli said she would try to go home. Tom did not disagree with her wishes, simply saying he would go along with what she felt. Eli was crying less, and could concentrate on work matters more reasonably. However Tom was still her lifeline, and they spoke daily by mobile. After the terrible event Tom had taken Eli to see a doctor and he had prescribed certain medication for her. Some was to help her sleep and the other tablets were to help cope with the trauma. Initially Eli had to take both lots of pills regularly but slowly Tom had tried to wean her off the medication. Now she was able to go days without having recourse to taking the tablets.

Gerry was very relieved to see Tom and Eli were trying to help each other over this dreadful time, and he felt sure that neither of them could have been party to this egregious slaying. Shirley, Eli and Tom had been very close when Shirley was alive why should Eli and Tom not remain close friends. Gerry, knowing Tom like he did, had no doubt that there was zero chance of him taking advantage of Eli.

At the next meeting between George and Chap, just a couple of weeks after the horrific slaying of Shirley. As would be expected, Chap was asking about the dreadful incident and George was reiterating what he had been told. As he had no personal experience of the tragedy. Chap was horrified by the egregious murder, and said he was sorry for the family and friends of Shirley, who must be finding it hard to cope with the loss. Everybody in town was absolutely shocked by this terrible event, George said, and it would take some time for the people to recover. It seemed as if everybody was looking behind them to see if they were being followed. George showed Chap the sales figures for the past three months and Chap was quick to notice an upturn in the monthly turnover. He commented on this to George, and asked if he had noticed any reason for this. George said "there had been an incident at the other pub on the north side." "Two fellows had a disagreement, over a woman, which escalated until a number of the patrons there began punching one another, and started throwing bar stools around." The police had been called, and eventually order was restored. The damage to the bar had been significant, and the owners were not happy. The two instigators were subsequently charged, and three or four patrons were banned for a couple of months for getting involved in the ruckus. All this caused quite a few of the more genteel patrons to come over to "George's Pub" because things were less stressful, and disruptive there. Plus George would not stand for violence of any sort. Talking about aggressive people made George think of Spider and Danny, he mentioned that Spider and Danny had not been in for a number of weeks, but he was not really missing them, and strangely of late, Rodney seemed somewhat subdued, but it did not stop him drinking, if anything he was drinking more. Chap finished his black label told George things were looking good and bid him good night and left.

Gerry knew a solicitor in the city who was known to have some shady characters as clients, so he phoned him to see if he could get some feedback on Shirley's murder. The lawyer was cagey, and Gerry knew straight away, he knew more than he was letting on. Gerry did not have any leverage at the moment, but he was sure something would come to light shortly. He would bide his time with Jim Cotter, the solicitor, who would be phoning for some or other favour, and then he would be ready for him. However Jim had admitted to Gerry that he was the solicitor for Shane Reynolds, one of the gang supposedly, involved in the shooting in the city. How this might affect anything to do with Shirley's murder, was anybody's guess. Gerry felt certain that Jim could divulge more about the shootings if he was obliged to.

Meanwhile things had stalled on both the gang killing in the city and the brutal murder of Shirley Edwards. The police could not catch a break, in spite of having 30 officers on the task full time. Spider and Danny were not doing so well either, Spider had assaulted one of the patron's of the "Mews Pub" they now used as their base, and was sentenced to three months community service However this still did not give Danny an opportunity to head south as Spider was there all the time. Since moving to Eden, Spider had been able to do a couple of "jobs" without ending up in jail. However being convicted was not all bad news, as word got around that he was an enforcer and this could lead to some more "work".

****

A newcomer to Tegwans' Nest arrived, having bought 10 acres of land. He, Rudy by name was of mediterranean decent, and said he was a chemical engineer from the big city and wanted to plant olive trees to produce olive oil. He engaged someone, with an earth moving monster, to the site. He instructed the fellow to construct rows of mounds of the top soil running down the slope with walk ways in between. The olive plants would be planted in the mounds allowing a certain distance between plants. The rows were about two and a half metres apart. He was of the opinion that the annual rainfall for the district, would be more than adequate to grow the trees. He arrived with a trailer load of small olive trees and proceeded to plant them as he had planned. Next he brought in water, in mobile tanks, to get the trees started. Things were going well, the trees were starting to grow. It was at this stage when things were progressing well that his wife got sick.

Nobody knew exactly what her malady was, but in a matter of weeks she passed away. Rudy was devastated, and lost all interest in the project. He very seldom came north now to tend his orchard. He had two young sons to raise and his situation did not improve, although the olive trees continued to grow. After a further year, the property was put on the market at a ridiculously high price, described as a business ready to be operated. However there were no takers. Later on he was forced to reduce the asking price a number of times, until it almost became reasonable. It was eventually sold but the locals were never told for how much.

THIRTEEN

Natalie had become quite proficient in her new job, as she was happy there and was concentrating on improving her skills to get ahead. One day George asked Jack to take some forms up to Gerry, for his attention. At the offices Natalie came to the front counter to see what she could do to help him. Jack was instantly struck by how attractive Natalie was. He explained who he was and what he was doing there, and Natalie appeared very comfortable dealing with him. Jack asked if he could come back for the forms the following day, and Natalie said that would be in order. The following afternoon Jack was back and Natalie immediately made herself available to talk to him. Jack was desperate to see more of Natalie so he asked her out on a date, and to his delight she said yes. Jack was over the moon with excitement. He rushed back to his dad to ask for Friday evening off as he had met the most wonderful girl and he wanted to date her. George smiled and said "yes and treat her well". Romance was in the air.

Unfortunately things were not going very well for Rodney. Something seemed to have gotten under Rodney's skin and he was on tender hooks expecting to be hauled in by the police, at any time and be interrogated. This had the effect of Rodney drinking more heavily, and paying less attention to his work. However things would get a lot worse for Rodney.

The big city police were waiting for the Bulls (the gang that had lost a member) to retaliate, it was just a matter of time. Four months after the horrific murder of Shirley Edwards, there was a gang shooting in the city. The gang known as the Bulls were out to get revenge for the shooting of one of their members. The Bulls devised a devious scheme in the form of a major drug deal. They had a disgraced ex cop, who had been discharged from the police for suspected drug deals, to throw in his lot with them. The ex cop, Karl Wessel, suggested he tell the Dogs he had a ton of 98% pure heroin coming in if they were interested. The Dogs were unaware of his affiliation with the Bulls, so when contacted by Karl Wessel offering a deal for 98%

pure heroin they were very interested.

The Dogs, were not prepared to let such a chance slip through their hands. Karl said he would be at the old disused, police station along May street on the following evening at 11pm if they were interested. They decided to attend with plenty of fire power in case the deal turned sour. What they did not know was it was an elaborate setup, by the Bulls, to extract revenge for the loss of their member four months earlier. One of the Bulls gang was sent to the old police station in the afternoon of the planned ambush to keep watch, to ensure the Dogs did not attempt a counter ambush. The instigators of this ambush had seven armed men, one with a rifle, and the rest with revolvers positioned around the meeting place, with each shooter able to view the scene of the impending drama without being seen. The rifleman was secreted in a trough, near a tap, which was deep enough for him to be unseen and 20 paces, at right angles to the path the member of the Dogs gang would walk. This trough was not visible from a distance, because of the slope of the ground. His task was to take out the Dogs negotiator when Karl Wessel raised his right hand.

The Dogs believed if they could score this deal, then they would be putting one over the Bulls. Shane had been a member of this gang for over ten years, and was feared by his adversaries. He was capable of terrible revenge against someone, who crossed him. Arriving with eight fellow members in two cars he checked out the scene from a block away, the venue was an old disused police station. Shane took his time, he had a Derringer pistol strapped to his right ankle and a flick knife taped to his left forearm. He got out of the car looked around, and all he could see was a lone figure waiting for him down the side of the building. The whole area was silent and deserted, and Shane did not think it was a set up. The guy he was going to deal with was a disgraced ex cop, who had been discharged for supposed drug deals, that could not be proven. Shane did not feel uncomfortable about this meeting as he had done some research on the ex cop, and found the story quite plausible. So he approached Karl Wessel waiting down the side of the building. As he got closer he could see the figure was holding a package in his right hand, which presumably, was a sample of the pure heroin that he had to trade.

When Shane got close enough to talk to the ex-cop, he asked if the parcel was a sample of what was available. As the ex cop raised his hand with the parcel in it, a shot rang out from a rifle and Shane died in the arms of the ex cop, who held Shane as a human shield between himself and Shane's accomplices waiting in the cars. All hell broke lose, with the gangsters in the cars at a serious disadvantage, as the opposition just rained bullets down on the cars. The Dogs were shooting wildly not knowing where the attack was coming from. The cars containing the gang members, were forced to leave the scene with a screeching of tyres. There was a good possibility that some of the occupants of the cars were injured. The hijackers put a further shot into the base of Shane's skull and left him there, retrieving the spent cartridges and disappeared. In five minutes everybody had disappeared except for Shane, who was lying in the yard of the deserted police station. In a further 15 minutes the police arrived, to a homicide with no witnesses. It did not take the police long to realise this was a gang murder, quite possibly in retaliation for the death of the gang member a few months back. One of the police recognised Shane as a member of the Dogs gang. Forensics arrived, and scouted around trying to understand how the event had occurred. At the scene of the murder the police found nothing. The perpetrators had even picked up the spent cartridges from the rifle.

An article appeared in the local newspaper in Emerald the following morning, stating that a suspected gang member Shane Reynolds had been shot dead, in an ambush at a disused police station in May Street in the big city. Gerry had the newspaper delivered to his home, and he read the article at the breakfast table. This incident gave Gerry something to think about. At work Gerry spent some time thinking about what he could make of this gang murder. Eventually he decided to phone Jim Cotter, the lawyer in the city, that had some dealings with the gang members. The police in Emerald had nothing to say about the killing, in the city. Next day Gerry phoned Jim Cotter, and asked about the gang murder. Jim sounded a bit down, and Gerry asked what was wrong and Jim mentioned the Shane had been one of his clients. Gerry asked if he thought this murder would result in all out war, and Jim replied that he did not think so, as each gang had lost one member and the others really wanted to stay alive, and pursue their drug activities. Gerry asked if it would be a big funeral but Jim replied he did not know, but it was being held in two days at 11am. at Westbrook Cemetery. Gerry asked if he had heard any more about the shooting in Emerald, and Jim said he had heard nothing. Gerry thanked Jim and terminated the call. Gerry sat thinking for a while, and then looked on the internet where Westbrook Cemetery was and how long it would take get there. Gerry called in his personal secretary, and enquired about his appointments for two days time. He asked her to reschedule the appointments as he was being called away, and he would not be in at all that day.

FOURTEEN

On the day, Gerry told his wife, Bev he would be going to the city and would be back by about 5pm. He left taking a pair of binoculars with him and drove down the eastern highway to the City. The journey was without incident but once in the city, traffic was very slow by Emerald standards. He made his way to the Westbrook Cemetery and got there at about 10.45am. Gerry did not know if he would see anybody he knew, so he parked the car half a block from the cemetery. He got out of the car taking his binoculars, which were in a small man's bag and slowly approached the cemetery trying to keep some trees between him and the people that had gathered to pay their respects to Shane. He estimated that there were about 25 mourners and of those about 15 were obviously bikies. He stood near some trees close to the mourners, but apart. He had to be reasonably close if he was hoping to recognise anybody. He studied the group trying to see if he recognised anyone.

His gaze fell on a tall thin fellow standing a little apart from the family. This guy did not look at all comfortable, in a suit. At a guess this was probably the second time in his life he was obliged to wear one. He believed he knew this individual, he had seen him around Emerald but not recently. After the ceremony, people started to leave and Gerry saw this thin character, who he believed he recognised, talking to a shortish thickset man with thinning hair, and wearing specs. Gerry could not allow this opportunity slip away, so he moved as close as he dared, and snapped a shot of the two of them, and moved away from the area. Back in his car Gerry looked at the photo on his mobile and was quite pleased with the results. Suddenly there was a knock on the car window, and Gerry looked up to see two men in suits.

He lowered the window, and they asked him for some form of identity. Having produced his drivers licence, they then asked what his interest was in the funeral. Gerry did not think it a good idea to lie to the two detectives, so he said he was a criminologist, and was gathering information and ideas for his book. They appeared to consider this for a moment, and then moved off. Gerry was much relieved to see them go. Although Gerry spoke to Jim Cotter on the phone he had never met him, but for some unknown reason, he was wondering if the man in the snapshot might be him. As everybody left Gerry saw the thin fellow get into a Subaru driven by someone he could not see properly, because of the sun shinning on the windscreen. After this Gerry went to his sister's home to see his sister and mother. He had lunch with them and sat talking to them for about an hour before returning home without incident.

Next morning at work, Gerry was thinking how he could find out who the thin man in the photo was when he had an idea "ask the publican". Most people visit the pub at some time or other, so there was a possibility George might know. If Gerry went to the police to ask who he was they would want to know why, the same with his friends, he did not want to ruffle any feathers. At lunch time Gerry went down to "George's Pub", sat down in the private bar, and George came over and greeted him, Gerry ordered a beer for himself and one for George. They exchanged pleasantries and then Gerry showed George the photo on his mobile, and asked if he knew who the tall individual was. George looked at it for a few moments, and said it was Spider Kelly, and he added that he had not been around for some considerable time. Now Gerry could remember him, a disgusting individual with no respect or regard for anybody. Someone who was far more comfortable in jeans and a denim jacket. Why would Spider Kelly go to Shane Reynolds funeral? Gerry finished his beer,told George the premises were looking very welcoming and left.

Jack, hurried over to the hotel to tell his mum about the lovely girl he had met, and who he had asked to go out with him. His mum was impressed, and reminded him to treat her like a lady. Jack assured his mum, that he would always do that. Back in the pub Jack told his dad and Peter about the lovely girl he met at Mr. Keane's offices and how he had asked her out on a date. Now Jack could phone Natalie back, and see if she was okay for Friday. Jack picked up Natalie at 6.30pm on Friday and for a few minutes they discussed what they would like to do. Natalie suggested getting "take away," and going down to the shores of the lake, to enjoy it there. Jack really liked that idea, so off they went. They found a quiet spot where they could sit down on the lawn, and have the fish and chips, and talk about each other. Natalie said she was an ordinary girl who was happy with family and friends, and was not really interested in glitz and glamour. Jack responded by saying he was not that way inclined either. By the time they had finished their meal they had found quite a few mutual interests. Natalie had explained that her dad, had walked out on her mum when she was just a little girl, and now her mum was crippled with arthritis so she helped her mum as much as she could. By the time Jack took Natalie home he was very impressed with his date and told her so. Jack asked if he could see her again, and Natalie said yes. On arriving back home Jack sought his mum, to tell her how the evening had been. It became obvious in a matter of minutes that Jack was smitten with Natalie, and he had to recount most the evening to his mum before he would allow her to go to bed. It looked as if the love bug had bitten Jack.

The following morning Rodney got a call from a Det. Sgt. Bert Lowe asking him to come down to the police station to see him as soon as possible. Rodney had a very dry throat all of a sudden, and could hardly answer the detective but he managed to say in a squeaky voice he could come down at 2pm that afternoon. Who was Det. Sgt. Bert Lowe, and what did he want with Rodney? The morning passed very slowly for Rodney, and by afternoon he was a wreak, so on his way to his appointment he stopped in at "George's Pub" for a vodka or two. On his arrival he told the constable on desk duty who he was, and that he had an appointment with Det. Sgt. Bert Lowe for 2.00pm. He was shown to a seat in the interview room, and told the detective would be with him shortly. The interview room was set up so the two persons using it would be seated at the short ends of the rectangular table. Thus ensuring that Rodney would be unable to see any notes Sgt. Lowe was making.

Now the nerves were beginning to play up, and he could not stop shaking. The detective concerned was observing Rodney through a one way window from the adjoining room, and wondered what Rodney was so nervous about. He let Rodney stew for a further 15 minutes, and then entered the room. He introduced himself to Rodney shaking his sweaty hand, and sat down. Bert Lowe feigned ignorance, and asked Rodney what he did, and where he did it? Rodney was not finding this easy, having kept him waiting this cop was pretending he knew nothing about him. Meanwhile he was sure this guy had sourced all the information he could on him. His mouth was completely dry again, and in spite of his best efforts Rodney, did not come across well. He had difficulty remembering facts about his job, and broke into a sweat, saying it was very hot in the room so Bert offered to adjust the air conditioning for him.

However this did not really stop him sweating, as Bert asked him if he knew an Estelle Brown. (This is not what Rodney expected, and there was a noticeable relaxation of Rodney's posture) Rodney said she was one of his clients in a divorce case, so Bert asked how it was going, Rodney replied that these things take time, as there are quite a number of issues to work through. Bert asked how long he thought it would still take, and Rodney said he was progressing it as fast as he could, as he did with all his cases. Bert said they (the police) had an interest in Estelle Brown, and they would be happy if she was given the best possible service. Now this was not true, but Rodney had no way of finding this out, Bert just wanted to put the fear, up Rodney. All the way through this interview Bert was making copious notes, Rodney was too far away to see exactly what Bert was writing. Bert ended the interview by saying they would be interested in seeing how Ms Brown's case progressed, and would be in touch. Sgt. Lowe's notes turned out to be a lot of squiggles making no sense, he had it all on tape.

Rodney nearly ran from the police station, and

Det. Sgt. Lowe watched with a grin on his face. Rodney needed a drink, and proceeded post haste to "George's Pub" where he ordered a double vodka and a beer. He went to a seat near the window where he felt he would be left to his thoughts. George was watching this with interest he had not seen Rodney this jittery before. Something or someone must have rattled his cage. Rodney could not fathom how the cop knew about Estelle Brown, surely she did not go to the police. Fortunately he had not brought up the question of payment, with Estelle, and now he will have to suggest something mundane like child minding, in lieu of money. This is not what he had in mind. Why were the cops harassing him, he had done nothing wrong.

Sgt. Lowe had learned that Rodney had more pressing things on his mind than Mrs. Brown. The Estelle Brown issue was not what Rodney feared there had to be something else. When Rodney answered the first couple of questions he seemed to relax a bit, suggesting that he had anticipated something else. Although he was still sweating it was not to the same degree. At this stage he had done nothing wrong in the Ms. Brown divorce case, so why was he sweating so profusely. There had to be something else haunting him, for Rodney to be in panic mode. He had quite obviously been involved in something far more serious, than trying to force Ms. Brown into a compromising situation. Sgt. Lowe was keen to have a chat with Sgt. Lewis about Rodney, as something was not right.

Tom was still grieving Shirley's passing but he knew the only way to regain his equilibrium was to keep as busy as possible. He had been scouting around for premises that might suit his solar power project, and had found a disused plant that might just do the job, the only drawback was it was in north Emerald, and his other business was in south Emerald. He had been hoping to have them closer together. Next time Tom and Gerry got together Tom mentioned the fact that he could not find any premises near his security business, to hire, and he might be forced to go to north Emerald. Gerry responded that he had just been dealing with a firm, a few doors down from Tom, that was being forced to relinquish their premises, as they were in financial strife, and they needed someone to take over their lease of the building. As this was not common knowledge yet Gerry told Tom to phone Brad Smith the fellow concerned, and say that Gerry had suggested Tom contact him concerning the lease of the building. Tom immediately phoned

Brad, and explained that Gerry had told him the premises might be available.

FIFTEEN

They made arrangements to meet at Brad's business, to see if they could negotiate a deal. Tom and Brad arrived at the premises at the same time, and they introduced themselves, and went inside so Tom could gauge the size of the interior. He looked around, and saw the building would be a little big, but that would allow for expansion. There was plenty of light from the big windows, and the working area was clean and free of any oil stains. There was a big roller door at the east end of the building which could allow a truck to be kept inside overnight. Brad mentioned that the two offices in the front of the building were soundproofed. This was good as it would ensure that office staff, would be able to use their mobiles without concern about any noise from the workshop. The restroom facilities were clean and stain free. These premises could not be very old Tom thought, and Brad confirmed this. Tom was very pleased with what he saw, and hoped that they would be able to make a deal on the rental of the premises. However he did not let on to Brad how keen he was on obtaining the site. The premises were ideal for the solar project, all Tom said to Brad was that the premises might be right, and he would need to discuss the deal with Mr. Keane. Brad said that he was keen to vacate the premises in one month. Tom said that time line would suit him, and he would be prepared to take over the lease provided his accountant approved of the conditions, and this could be accomplished in the next week, Brad was noticeably relieved.

In the course of the next week the paperwork was signed for Tom to take over the premises in one months time. He was very pleased with the arraignments, and on meeting Eli after work he told her all about the plan to take over the new premises. She was excited, and asked to see the facilities. So Tom took her past the building saying, when he received the keys he would take her through the premises. Eli was glad to be included in the things Tom did. It gave her a feeling of belonging, something she had lacked at home, never being taken into confidence by her father. This was something new in her life, brought about by Tom and his special treatment of her. Eli was beginning to feel very comfortable in Tom's company. It was now nine months since Shirley's brutal murder, and no word of any progress. When Tom and Eli would visit Shirley's dad, Don, to see how he was doing he would display a stiff upper lip about her demise, and say to Tom that it would be right if he and Eli could be together.

Tom was very keen on Eli but felt, it was too soon after Shirley's murder to take any steps to further their relationship as it would reflect badly on Eli. Shirley would remain forever in his heart but life has to go on, and he believed that Shirley would be happy if he and Eli married. In life there are two sets of rules, one for males and one for females. The males, it seems, cannot tarnish their names as all would be forgiven,- Why?- Nobody knows. However in the case of a female, things are different, there are definite does and don'ts. Should a female disrespect these norms and customs then there will be consequences. She will be regarded by the public, as an example of what not to do, and be shunned by many as a pariah. Being seen with Tom now is no different to the way it was when Shirley was still around, unless it is all the time. Being married to Tom inside two years would create an absolute scandal which would make life very unpleasant for Eli. They both considered Emerald to be their home so they were not about to pull up sticks and move elsewhere. So they would remain in Emerald, and try as best they could to conform to the norms of society.

One evening after Eli and Tom had a barbecue at Tom's house. They sat talking about where they were going Tom told Eli that he could not envisage himself without her, as she was part of his life now, and he was hoping to marry her, if she would have him. Eli responded by saying that nothing would give her greater pleasure, and she looked forward to the day. Their relationship had changed, and become personal since the passing of Shirley, and they were grateful for that. So they would continue to see each other, as much as possible while ignoring the scandal mongers. The only one walking in Tom's shoes was he, and he was not going to tarnish Eli's reputation. Tom explained the double standards of society regarding the behaviour of men, and women, and Eli said she was aware of the situation, and would wait till it was acceptable for them to get married. In the meantime their relationship was growing ever stronger.

Jack was feeling ten foot tall, he had arranged

another date with lovely Natalie and had asked if he might meet her mother. Natalie thought that was a very nice idea, and said she would arrange it with her mum. On the day in question Jack arrived with a beautiful bouquet of flowers for Mrs. Stokes, and Natalie took him inside to meet her mum. Jack saw a lady, crippled and bent with arthritis, in a wheelchair, smiling up at him, and he greeted her, and presenting her with the bouquet. Well this sure put Jack in Mrs. Stokes good books, she could not remember when last she received a bouquet from anyone. They made general conversation, and Jack told Mrs. Stokes that she had a wonderful daughter. This was not fake, Jack was a gentleman, and he asked Mrs. Stokes if they could bring anything back for her.

She said she did not require anything at present, and Jack and Natalie went off. From the time they left, Natalie was just beaming all the way down to the restaurant and Jack said "what is going on"? Natalie replied "he had just become her mother's fan for life". "Your mother is a very courageous lady, and deserves much more than we can give her"Jack said. They had a meal at Ocean restaurant and then walked along the lakeside chatting about what they would like to achieve in life. They got a takeaway coffee at Risto's, and sat down on one of the benches alongside the lake to watch the sunset. The two of them were not movie lovers, and preferred the outdoors. Natalie told Jack how her father left them when she was just a little girl, and how her mum battled on with her arthritis, which was slowly getting worse. Natalie left school after year 10. She went to work as a "check out chick" at Rolfe's Supermarket during the day, and attended Tafe at night to get a secretarial diploma. Then she went to work for Rodney Pleasant, as his secretary until she could no longer put up with his abuse. She was then fortunate enough to see an advert in the local newspaper, for a secretarial position with "Keane and Associates". She applied and Mr. Keane interviewed her, and offered her the position which she gladly accepted, and she was very happy there as Mr. Keane looked after his staff. Jack asked if Rodney did not look after his staff, and Natalie responded that she had been the only member of staff, and Rodney had treated her badly. Natalie elaborated on Rodney's treatment of her, and Jack was quite upset on hearing what she had to say. So she made Jack promise not to go after Rodney. Natalie said "through all of this her mother came first."

Sgt. Bert Lowe and Sgt. Fred Lewis had a little chat about Rodney Pleasant, Bert was concerned that Rodney was hiding something he was extremely scared of. He showed Fred some of the video he had taken of Rodney on the day he came in for an interview with Bert. It was very obvious that Rodney, had the shakes, and it was not about the Estelle Brown case. His expression changed, and he swallowed and relaxed a bit, when he heard her name mentioned, because he had not yet propositioned her, about her payment for the divorce case. He was not worried about that so what could it be? Fred said he was unaware of anything else going on that could have caused such fear. After further discussion it was decided they would both make more enquiries, through their informants and meet again soon.

Tom engaged an electrician Brian Donald who started work on the day Tom took over the premises. It was preferable that Brian was there on day one to organise the shop as he saw fit, being the one that would be in charge. Brian was the right man for this position and Tom had confidence he would thrive in this role, as he had very good reports on Brian's abilities. Now Brian and Tom discussed the purchase of work benches and Tom ordered them to be delivered the next day. Once the work benches had arrived and been installed to Brian's liking, leaving space for a truck to be driven into the workshop by way of the roller door on the east end of the building. Tom said Brian should source two installers to start the following Monday. Brian said this was no problem as he had two individuals in mind already. This pleased Tom as it showed Brian was thinking ahead. Tom made arrangements through a leasing company for a truck suitable to their requirements. So he and Brian went down to collect the truck the following day and they collected some ladders from the hardware store before returning. Tom and Brian made up the first order of panels, rails and fittings for the first two jobs that was already in the pipeline. Tom showed Brian which suppliers to use and which ones to avoid. Tom believed he needed to use the best products to ensure his customers would end up with a system that was going to provide the best results for the client. Using cheap parts would only result in many complaints and claims, something Tom was very keen to avoid. He had been very busy putting out flyers about the solar power systems and contacting his existing customers to let them know that solar power was readily available. He asked Eli if she would help by ordering some office furniture he had shown her in a catalogue and then see about some pot plants to spruce up the office area as she saw fit. Eli really appreciated Tom asking her to help, as it made her feel part of the event. Eli was impressed with the facilities for the solar business and said so to Tom. He was happy to hear she was interested in the project and liked the factory. With the new premises and a staff under Brian Donald's leadership Tom was confident they were starting off on the right foot with the solar business. Letting Brian organise his crew the way he saw fit would give him confidence in his ability. He would just keep an eye on the progress to see how it worked out. He had impressed on Brian the need for being at the work site at the time prearranged so that the customer could feel confident in their word. Furthermore it was very important that the installers knew exactly what they needed to do, once they arrived on the job. If the guys stood around as if uncertain of their task this would not look very professional to the home owner.

Tom had completed the registration papers for "Emerald Solar". As a registered electrician one of Brian's jobs was to check the work of the installers before connecting the system to the inverter. Once this was done the home owner was required to notify his energy supplier that he was ready to receive solar power. The energy company would then dispatch an electrician to do the final connecting to the meter and the solar system would become active. Tom said based on what they had ordered in the way of components Brian should prepare an order for sufficient parts to do a further ten homes and submit the order, this way they would keep ahead of the projects to be done. Although orders to the suppliers were supposed to be delivered in a week, this was not always the case, and Tom was not about to let a customer down. Doing so would cause him to get a name as being, unreliable. Tom had built his security business on reliability, and his idea was to do the same with Emerald Solar.

The plan was Brian would show his guys, how to assemble the racks, and then attach the panels to the racks, in the workshop so that when they get on the client's roof, they would know what to do. It was essential that the applicants were not afraid of heights. Brian would interview the applicants for the job according to what he expected from them. The first applicants would be coming in the next couple of days. On the sales front Tom, had two homeowners keen on having solar power installed, so Tom was keen to get this happening so there would be an example for any prospective client to see. He took Brian around to the two sites so he would have an idea of what to expect. Tom said the business would be known as Emerald Solar, and he got on the phone to arrange for a time and day when the decals would be attached to the vehicles doors. Having the truck inside the factory would facilitate the loading of the components in the mornings. Then the crew would be ready to head off to the next job. Brian was given a company mobile so he was readily available, and then Tom left him to carry on while he went back to Edwards Security up the road.

SIXTEEN

Shortly after the interview between Rodney and Bert, Gerry turned up at the police station to see Fred. While they were talking about the programme for the wayward youth, Fred happened to mention the incident with Rodney, when he was being interviewed by Bert. He asked Gerry if he had any idea why Rodney would be so terrified of being questioned by the police. Gerry said he could not think of anything at the moment, but said he would give it some thought. On leaving the police station Gerry went back to his office where he sat thinking. He was not aware of any incident that had occurred in Emerald over the last year, other than Shirley's horrific murder, could Rodney have anything to do with that? How could that be? Rodney would be too scared to fire a hand gun at someone, and if he did he would miss. Maybe Rodney knew who had shot Shirley. That would give him cause for concern, and

Rodney was very concerned right now.

When Jack got home from his date, the same ritual occurred he sought out his mum, and gave her a full account of the lovely evening he had spent with Natalie. Teresa could see Jack was very keen on Natalie, and just said to him to go slowly, as she did not want him to get hurt. For Jack life just revolved around his dates with Natalie, after one, he was already getting set for the next one. George sat talking to Jack one day before they opened for business, and pointed out that he needed to think about what he would do if things got very serious with Natalie. He obviously had shares in the hotel and pub but which way would he like to go. Jack responded that he had thought about it a bit, and there were a number of issues. Firstly Natalie's mum was in a wheelchair crippled with arthritis, and at the moment she is quite dependant on Natalie. Secondly he did not have a lot of money saved, and thirdly if they were destined to marry how would that affect his position in the family and the business.

Life in Eden was not without it's moments. Every little while, Spider would lay into someone, off the pub premises, to avoid being barred, and then things would go quiet for a while. The thing was that Spider was getting a name for his violent behaviour and Danny was worried it might result in both of them going to prison. Spider realised trying to run his drug business from Eden did not make sense. They were on the road most of the day between Emerald and Eden trying to keep up with demand. They needed to return to Emerald as soon as possible.   It was now over a year since Shirley's horrific murder and the informants were not talking, either they were too scared to talk, or they knew nothing.

Emerald Solar was coming along nicely, once some systems had been installed, people became more interested and the business was thriving. Tom was happy with the progress, and the way Brian Donald was running the developing solar business, and felt sure that it would only get busier. Tom was running adverts in the local news, and had held an information evening at the local hall. Those present showed plenty of interest in what he had to say. After the event a number of people asked for a quote for a system on their homes. This would lead to further installations, as the price of electricity continued to increase.

Gerry did not have many close friends, but he did have many acquaintances, some more reputable than others, and the more shady ones did not know anything in relation to Shirley's dreadful murder. Gerry was at a complete loss as to know what happened on that fateful afternoon. All his efforts to garner some information had resulted in absolutely nothing. He was beginning to think that the only persons who knew something were the shooter and possibly Rodney, and poor Rodney was very, very scared. Gerry so wanted to help his friends Tom, and Eli find some sort of closure to this dreadful event. He knew for sure that Tom was still hurting badly, over the despicable murder of his wife, Shirley. Although Tom and Eli were very close now, that did not mean that Tom had no more feelings for Shirley. Tom needed closure, so did Eli, this would only truly come with the solving of the mystery around her death.

Natalie and Jack were getting on very well and were seeing each other a few times a week. Jack often turned up as she finished work and they would go back to her mum's house where Jack could do no wrong. He would spend time with Mrs. Stokes talking about the crochet work she had around the house and the little canary perched on the rung inside his cage where he happily whistled away. While Natalie was out, Bill (the canary) was her company, helping her get through the day. Jack made a point of getting "take away" sometimes and going back to enjoy a meal with Natalie and her mum so she would not be alone. Natalie really appreciated Jack's attention to her mum. Although they had not discussed their future together as yet, Jack was having serous discussions with his father, George. As to what his position might be should he and Natalie get married.

George assured Jack that he would always be his son and marrying Natalie would only make the family bigger. Jack said that should he and Natalie get married they might live in the house with her mum initially as she could not be left alone 24/7, that would be inhumane. Through all of this Peter was highly amused, how Jack had fallen head over heels for Natalie. He had never imagined that Jack could change overnight, on meeting Natalie. Peter liked Natalie and thought she was a lovely girl and wished them all the best. Now he was a little apprehensive about what might befall himself. George pointed out that Jack's job at the bar was safe, and nobody was going to oust him. Furthermore whatever happened in the future they would work around it. One evening after being out for a meal, Jack brought Natalie home to meet his family and the consensus of opinion was that she was a lovely girl, good looking and practical. All the family were happy to meet Natalie and Jack was very glad to see his mum and sister, Michele get on well with her. It was early days yet and the two love birds had to go slowly before making any decisions. They all agreed that her early childhood did not seem to have done her any harm, if anything it had strengthened her character. Jack knew whatever decisions he and Natalie took they would have to bear Natalie's mum in mind.

Chap and George were having one of their regular meeting in the private bar of "George's Pub". The latest figures pleased Chap, and he enquired how the family was doing, George explained that Jack was now dating Natalie Stokes a young lady working for Gerry Keane from the accounting firm of the same name. He felt that since taking over the ownership of the bar and hotel they had improved, and were now capable of running the bar with two full time persons, so maybe one of them should be bringing in money on another project. George realised they were not highly skilled, but they were keen workers and not afraid of a challenge. Chap suggested George talk to his accountant about this issue as Chap said he had no problem with the idea, as to date they had repaid 95 percent of their loan which was excellent, and provided the hotel did not suffer he thought it a very good idea.

SEVENTEEN

The next day George made an appointment to see Gerry, and arriving at 2 pm. as agreed. He explained the reason for his visit saying he had raised the idea, of the family looking for an additional small business to supplement their hotel and bar. Chap thought that it was worthy of pursuing, to see if anything was available. Gerry said it was an excellent idea and pulled George's file to check the progress they had made with the repayment on the hotel and bar. Gerry had to agree that George and family had done extremely well repaying 95 percent of the loan in the years they had the business. George said he had been talking to the owner, of the bakery they get their bread, pies, buns, cakes etc. from, Olaf Jurgens, who seemed to be thinking of retiring. If this was a financial proposition then it might be worth their while to acquire it, and run it in conjunction with the hotel and bar. They would have better control of the bread and pastries and be able to provide the hotel according to it's needs cutting out the middle man. Gerry agreed, but said it would depend very much, on the asking price for the business. Gerry did the bakery's books so he was able to see the turnover, and said if they made the baker a reasonable offer now he might accept it as it saved the trouble of putting it on the market and having to wait and see if there were any interested parties. George was keen to do this if Gerry thought it a viable proposition. George was thinking of asking Jack to run the bakery, and supply the hotel and the public. Jack had learned a lot when standing in for his dad when required to, and he was level headed. Of course it would depend on whether the owner of the bakery would be willing to stay on for three months to show Jack how to bake, and run the shop. Gerry said he would juggle the figures and see what they could afford to pay for the bakery.

George went back to the pub and that evening, he got Jack and Peter to sit down with him and go through the idea of purchasing the bakery to run in conjunction with the hotel and bar. He explained the fact that the owner had mentioned to him that he was thinking of retiring. George asked Jack how he would feel about running a business on his own.

Jack said he would be delighted and give it his best shot. So George asked Jack to go over to the bakery the next day, and just have a look at the situation, see what he thinks, but say nothing to the owner. Jack was more than willing to do this as any progress was good progress according to Jack. The following day Jack went over to the bakery, and just had a look around and bought a pastry, Jack liked the idea. Back at the hotel he told his Dad that he liked the idea of the bakery, and he would be prepared to take it on.

Gerry got back to George the next day saying they should offer no more than $35,000 but should first draw the owner out to see what figure he was thinking of. George agreed that was the way to go, and the next afternoon just after lunch George and Jack went to the bakery ostensibly to buy a birthday cake for his wife, Teresa. George asked Olaf, "How long had he been running the bakery in North Emerald." Olaf said,"He had been running the bakery in Emerald for 45 years. The ovens were checked every three years and a certificate was issued, and all was in order." George enquired if he owned the building and Olaf replied, "he rented it on a four year term." "How much did Olaf wish to ask for the goodwill?" George asked, "Somewhere around $40,000 " Olaf replied. George thought about this for a while and then said. "I will give you $32000 if you will stay on to teach my son Jack how to make the bread. "Also I would like an extension of the building lease of four years. Olaf replied, "he could ask the owners regarding the extension of the lease. He would think about George's offer for the bakery and let him know in one week,"

Things were not going well for Spider and Danny. Life in Eden was not the same as in Emerald, it did not feel right and they were keen to come back to Emerald. There had been no swoop by the police desperately searching for someone to blame for Shirley's demise and now things were even quieter. So one afternoon they decided to just drive through and see how things were in Emerald. Spider instructed Danny to abide by all road rules so as not to draw attention to themselves. All went according to plan as they crossed the bridge and went down Little street and circled back to town centre,it felt good to be back in Emerald. Spider just wondered if it was truly quiet or if there was trouble brewing. They drove back across the bridge and Spider told Danny to stop at the bakery so they could get some meat pies. They parked a number of doors down from the bakery and Spider said he would go in and get the pies.

The old guy was not there but there was a young chick, standing at the counter. Spider moved up close to her and tried to put his arm around her and pull her close to him. Natalie reacted instantly shouting at him to let her go, Jack in the back of the bakery along with Olaf heard the commotion and rushed to the front of the store to see Spider assaulting Natalie. Jack wasted no time, pulling Natalie away to the left and sending a big right fist crashing into Spider's face breaking his nose and loosening a few front teeth. Spider hit the floor hard, unaware of his surroundings. Spider lay on the floor out for the count but Jack was not concerned for him, just for Natalie who was shaken up but not injured in any way. Meanwhile Danny had been sitting in his car watching events through a wing mirror, on the car. He rushed over, and helped get Spider up and dragged him away to his car.

Olaf got Natalie a glass of water, and was very concerned for her, but she assured him she was okay, just a little shaken up. Natalie said she did not want the assault to be reported to the police as it would make matters worse. Jack recognised Spider as a frequenter of "George's Pub" although he had not been around for a while. Olaf was most apologetic about the confrontation but Jack assured him it was not his fault.

Jack and Natalie left Olaf, telling him they would be back, and went over to "George's Pub" where Jack took Natalie into the private bar sat her down, and gave her a small brandy to settle her. George came to see that Natalie was okay. The rest of the family heard about the incident and came to see her and give her their support. George was not happy with the situation, as the last thing they needed was Spider wanting revenge, and in the process, scuttling the bakery deal. George got hold of Sgt. Lewis, and explained the incident to him, saying he was busy negotiating a deal with Ofal, and did not need a rogue like Spider upsetting the business.

Danny took Spider back to Eden and realised he needed to see a doctor, so he went straight to the emergency department at the hospital and they told the nurse Spider had fallen from a height when he got dizzy and landed on his face. He was seen by a doctor after a three hour wait. He was x -rayed and the Doctor told him he had a broken nose and three loose teeth in the upper jaw. The broken nose would heal in time and he should have the loose teeth extracted. However they did give him a script for pain pills. Spider and Danny returned to their digs. Spider was a very unhappy fellow, not only did he not see the punch coming but he did not see who threw the punch, and Danny claimed he did not see the scuffle. The doctor's report stated, Spider had suffered a serious blow to the face, fracturing his nose and loosening three teeth in the upper jaw, and these injuries were consistent with the individual being struck forcibly with a big fist.

Spider was pestering Danny, asking him who had struck him at the bakery, but Danny was adamant he did not see the guy so he could not tell him. Spider did not know whether to believe him or not so he just carried on nagging Danny, but there would be no confirmation of his assailant as Danny had decided enough was enough, the reign of terror had to stop. Spider was completely out of control. As soon as he had some drink and a zoll he would go looking for trouble it had to stop, Danny was becoming quite depressed with the situation and found it increasingly upsetting to be forced to drive Spider around. He was doing his best to get people, usually young ones, to try weed, and promising them, there was more where that came from. To date Danny had not found a way to escape from Spider's clutches, but he was constantly looking for an opportunity. The problem was if he tried and was unsuccessful he would be severely beaten by Spider or maybe even killed. So an attempt had to be undertaken only if he was reasonably sure of success. Danny was aware that Spider would be in a very uncomfortable position if he could engineer his escape. So Spider was being extra careful about keeping Danny where he could see him. The day they went down to the big city for Shane's funeral he even took the car keys away from Danny so he could not drive away while Spider was attending the ceremony at the graveside. All of this was playing on Danny's mind and he was finding the situation very difficult to deal with. If his mum was near, so he could talk to her, he felt sure she would be able to give him good advice. He was just hoping once they returned to Emerald, he would be given the chance to escape.

EIGHTEEN

Sgt. Lewis was very interested in Spider, wondering where he had been hiding for the last year plus. As Eden was not in the same police district as Emerald, there was no regular reporting and consultations between the police stations. Unfortunately, this had resulted in Spider's presence and misbehaviour in Eden not reaching the police in Emerald. Now Sgt. Lewis made his way back to the station having promised George he would look into the matter. He immediately contacted Sgt. Toms in Eden and enquired if he knew a fellow called Spider Kelly, Sgt. Toms replied, unfortunately he did, as he was on his patch, getting drunk and assaulting people. Sgt. Lewis said that Spider was being investigated regarding a number of incidents in the Emerald area and he would like to have any information about Spider since he moved to Eden. Sgt. Toms said he would be more than happy to oblige, and hoped that Sgt. Lewis would make arrangements to take Spider and his side kick Danny, although, he had done no wrong.

Gerry's property, had a row of big pines along it's western boundary. He felt he needed to support Tom's endeavours so he had the solar power installed along the roof on the eastern side of the house. He was quite delighted with the fact that it made a difference to the power bill. Tom had assured him it would. Tom and Gerry were sitting in the private bar at "George's Pub" having a beer after work. They had decided way back to get together about once a week and have a beer and talk about everything that might affect them or their families. This proved to be a sound approach as they now heard from George about the ruckus at the bakery, and how Jack had flattened Spider with one punch. Although Tom was not really interested in Spider, Gerry was, as he felt that somehow Spider had something to do with Shirley's death, but he did not know what. Gerry also told Tom he had heard from Sgt. Lewis, that Spider had been in Eden since he left Emerald at about the time of Shirley's death, and the police in Emerald were none the wiser as the two towns were in different police districts.

Tom was still very sore over Shirley' demise, but

drew great solace from Eli's company, and the two saw each on a daily basis. Without Eli's presence Tom could quite possibly have suffered a mental breakdown. In time Eli would get over the loss of Shirley, as women are more resilient, than most men. That did not mean that Eli did not need Tom, in fact she needed him quite desperately, as an anchor. Since the time Eli, and Tom had been thrust together, over the death of Shirley, they had become very close, and discussed most things. In fact Eli had been in on the solar power project right from the start. She was fully aware of the progress of the business, and felt a certain sense of pride, in the way solar power was accepted in Emerald. The team under, Brian Donald, were installing eight units over a two week period which was about the maximum they could achieve, as there were preparations to be made in the workshop before each installation. At this stage Tom and Eli did not want to do more, as it would require employing more staff and they were not ready to expand. The waiting list was between seven and 10 customers which was about what they hoped to keep it at. Tom wanted the team to feel comfortable with what they were doing, before employing more staff.

Rodney was not well. He was nervous, found it

difficult to sleep, and would jump at the slightest noise. In spite of his best endeavours, to convince himself that he was in the clear, he could not shake off a feeling of unease. He thought that somehow the police knew about his scheme, to oblige Estelle Brown to repay the debt for the divorce case, by way of a intimate relationship with Rodney. Although as yet he had not mentioned the idea to Estelle. If she had friends in the police then that idea was a no no, and he would be obliged to think of something else.

The police had looked carefully at Shirley's life, and there were no skeletons in the cupboard. Tom for his part was definitely not involved, his life was a clean slate. There were plenty of questions but no answers, someone, somewhere had to have some information. If so, why would they not come forward? Were they scared of being incriminated in Shirley's slaying?

Tom was comfortable leaving the job of finding Shirley's assassin to the police, as he had no expertise in this field. Gerry was not happy that the police would get to the bottom of the event, he was keen to make some enquiries of his own. He was confident that Spider was involved somehow, but there was also the nagging situation with Rodney. He was very definitely involved in something shady, his behaviour said that loud and clear, but what was it? Gerry did not think Rodney could be involved in Shirley's death.

Sgt. Lewis and Sgt. Lowe decided to get Rodney down to the station again to see if they could drag some information from him with regard to Shirley's death. The scene was set, Rodney was required to report to the police station at 2 pm sharp. On his arrival he was shown into interview room 1 where he could be observed through a one way window. They let Rodney stew for 20 minutes by which time he was in a heavy sweat. The two Sergeants. entered the room and apologised for keeping him waiting, saying they had just returned, from a raid on someone's property. Rodney did not know what to make of this, but it did not make him any more comfortable. He was physically trembling, and quite pale. Sgt. Lewis offered him a drink of water, coffee or tea but Rodney declined knowing full well he would not be able to raise the cup to his mouth, without spilling the contents.

The interview started slowly as the police asked how he was doing, and if his family were well. This really annoyed Rodney, why did they not get to the reason he was there. They asked how Mrs. Brown's divorce was proceeding, and if the case would be resolved in an equitable way. Rodney replied he was doing his best for her. Sgt. Lowe said they were very happy to hear that, and he would let the superintendent know, about the good progress of Estelle's divorce case. This only served to rattle Rodney's cage even more. (There was no Superintendent interested in Estelle Brown's divorce case.) The next question really got to Rodney, Sgt. Lewis asked how much he knew about Shirley Edwards' murder. It took Rodney a few minutes before he began to stammer that he knew nothing, about the death of Shirley Edwards. He placed his hands in his lap, as they were shaking so much. Sgt. Lowe asked him if he knew Spider, and Rodney's voice went all croaky as he denied he knew him. Sgt. Lewis replied that this could not be true, and he had a witness who saw him talking to Spider in "George's Pub" on more than one occasion. Rodney replied he might have just greeted him as one does, to other regulars of the pub he frequents. Sgt. Lowe countered, a few weeks before Shirley's death Rodney had got a drink in the pub, and then moved to the snooker room to talk to Spider. Now what could that have been about? Rodney had no memory of this event, and replied he had defended Spider on a couple of charges of assault, so this was probably in connection with one of those cases. Sgt. Lowe said, so you do know Spider? Rodney said only vaguely as a client. Sgt. Lewis said they would terminate the interview for now, and call him in again as needed. They now had further leads to pursue in the interim.

Rodney was completely exhausted and very happy to leave the police station, hurrying to "George's Pub" to get a beer and a double vodka. George served Rodney and saw him take the drinks to a corner table and sit down. He looked gaunt and frightened so George presumed he had received some bad news, in record time Rodney was back for the same again, so George kept an eye on him as he did not wish to be named as the landlord who allowed an inebriated patron to drive home.

When Rodney stopped drinking George told him Peter, his son, would drive him home. He told Peter to try, and find out what had upset him so. When Peter asked Rodney if he was all right. He started ranting about the police persecuting him, and saying he was responsible for Shirley's death. Peter said nothing he just listened as Rodney carried on about Sergeants. Lewis and Lowe accusing him of having something to do with the death of Shirley. Peter took Rodney to his front door pressed the bell, and left getting back to the bar in short time. He told George and Jack about Rodney's rantings, and they were very interested to hear what had been going on at the police station.

NINETEEN

The next day Tom and Gerry came in for their regular beer, and George brought them up to date on Rodney's dilemma, being persecuted by the Emerald police force. Gerry was of the opinion that there had to be some truth in it, if Rodney was reduced to a physical and mental wreck. If he was completely innocent then he would have told Sgt. Lewis and Sgt. Lowe to get lost he knew nothing. Tom was inclined to go along with that assessment, but he did not believe Rodney was more than a fringe player in the scheme, to eliminate Shirley. Rodney for his part felt the police were trying to pin Shirley's murder on him, as they had nobody else in their sights, and they were desperate to solve the case. Tom doubted Shirley knew Spider to talk to, but she might have known him by sight. Maybe Spider was the perpetrator, but surely somebody had put him up to it, as he could not have had a reason to kill her, other than perhaps for monetary gain or for drugs.

Later that evening Tom was bringing Eli up to date, about what had transpired that day, and Eli said she believed Shirley knew Rodney by sight although, she doubted they had ever spoken to each other. Then Eli remembered Shirley telling her, just a while before she was to lose her life, that Rodney had walked past her and tried to grab her hand to pull her to him, but Shirley had avoided his contact and told him, "get lost you pathetic weasel", before he could react she was out of sight. Tom found this interesting, and decided he needed to tell Gerry about this, as he might be able to make something of this. Tom assumed this fact had come out in the interview between Rodney and Sgt. Lewis and Sgt. Lowe so they would know about it. Next morning while talking to Gerry on some issues about the solar business, he told Gerry what Eli had told him the previous evening, about Rodney making a pass at Shirley, and her response. Gerry was intrigued by this news, and just thanked Tom for bringing him up to speed on the events. Now this made a bit of sense to Gerry, Rodney might have felt Shirley had insulted him, and he was out for revenge. But Gerry felt that Rodney just did not have the guts, to take it any further.

A week later, Olaf rang George to ask if he could come over after supper to have a chat and George said that would be good. He arrived about 7.30pm and George ushered him into the private bar, which was currently unoccupied. Olaf was impressed with the room and said so to George, and they sat down at one of the bigger tables, as Jack would be joining them shortly. George offered Olaf a brandy and he accepted, when the brandies for Olaf and George were produced Jack joined them at the table. Olaf said he had thought about the offer and knew that having to advertise the business for sale would take time and quite frankly he was tired, so he would accept an offer to buy the bakery at $33,000 if he was to teach Jack everything about the business over an extended period of time. George said he would accept that price. Further Olaf said as he was not going anywhere, he would be available to ensure that Jack knew what he was doing, as working with the ovens required a certain amount of expertise. George said the $33,000 was reasonable under the circumstances, and he would like to proceed with the deal as soon as possible.

Olaf said he was in full agreement to go ahead, so they should get Mr. Keane to draw up a contract with the Emerald Bakery going into Jack's name. George phoned Gerry the next morning, and gave him the deal details, and asked him if he could draw up a contract, which they would come and sign at his convenience.

Jack was keen to get into the job, so he was happy with the arrangements. He believed he would get on well with Olaf. He said it might take longer for Jack to understand all the tricks of the trade, but he would still be available to help Jack, as he was not going anywhere. Olaf said the offer was reasonable, and he was happy with it. Jack was very pleased to be able to get a chance, to show he was capable of this task. Jack felt that until now, he had been coasting, as the work in the pub was not exact mind blowing. Now he would be able to show his full potential, by operating a bakery on his own, and he had no fear of not being up to the task. He would make his mum and dad proud of him.

Tom was concerned about the idea, that Spider could have been asked to assault Shirley. He did not have any intention of mentioning this to Eli, as it would upset her very much. He would let it slide, and hope that nobody else would mention it in her company. Eli had made considerable progress in dealing with the loss of Shirley, the crying was less frequent, and not so intense, so Tom wanted her progress to continue in this vein. Their relationship was getting stronger every day, and this was of paramount importance to Tom, he did not wish to have to deal with another major emotional issue. Tom's make up, required him to have a very stable emotional attachment, in order for him to function as an effective member of society, anything less was extremely destabilising.

He had grown up in a household where the relationship he had with both his mother and father was loving, caring, compassionate and considerate, where trauma was not a common occurrence and he had flourished in this environment as his achievements up until he moved to Emerald, and even up to the dreadful day of Shirley's death, showed.

Now it was difficult to keep it all together, but it was coming right slowly with Eli's help, affection, and encouragement. Without realising it, Eli was in much the same position. From her earliest years at school Eli had learned to rely on Shirley. Unknowingly she had accepted Shirley as her mentor, as there was no father at home and her mother was so engrossed in trying to run the family home, while working as a cleaner. The contact between her mother and Eli was not adequate. So Shirley took up the task instinctively, by relaying to Eli what she had been told to do by her parents, and they usually did it together.

George, Jack and Olaf attended Gerry's offices two days later to sign the papers transferring the bakery into Jacks name, from the beginning of the following month, which was a week away. It was decided to put it straight into Jack's name, as otherwise further down the track the tax might become a problem for the family. The building owner had agreed to increase the term of rental for the premises, by a further four years, so George and family, were happy with the conditions. Jack appreciated the fact that he would have to be responsible for this venture, and make sure he learned the ropes quickly, his dad could not be his guardian angel any longer. Olaf said that Jack should become involved immediately, as there was no need to wait, and George thought this a good idea. Olaf said he would expect Jack to be at the bakery 5am every morning. Jack realised his life would be very different from now on. George had put down $25,000 on the deal, and Gerry had arranged the balance through Chap. Back at the hotel George, and the boys discussed the fact that Jack would not be available from the following morning. George and Peter felt that at present they could manage, if pushed they would see about getting a barmaid in. George, Estelle and Jack agreed that they would continue to run the bakery business as if Olaf was in charge. Once they had a better understanding the price of the pastries, and bread could be adjusted to suit their businesses.

TWENTY

As the two year anniversary of Shirley's death passed, Tom and Eli decided it was right for them to marry. The ceremony was low key with just Don and Gerry attending the court as witnesses to the event. Afterwards they went to Tom's home where they were joined by Beverley and Neve, as well, as a few friends from the Coffee and Sandwich Bar. Eli had known and worked with them, for a number of years. It was a very happy day for Eli, it was very pleasing to see her like that. Tom's reaction was a little more subdued, but he felt a contentment spreading over his being. Don and Gerry's family were very happy for them, and they all had a lovely time together. Don proposed a toast to Tom and Eli and said he was very happy, at their marriage and Shirley would be too. Gerry proposed a toast to Tom and Eli, and said this was the best thing that could happen. Both Tom and Eli were much more relaxed now, that the event was over, and they could get on with their lives. The couple spent 10 days, up the coast at a private resort, where they could not be harassed. Back in Emerald again they brought Eli's belongings, including her golden Labrador, Honey, over to Tom's house and Eli just beamed she was so happy. Eli had terminated the lease on the home she used to live in and thanked the owner for looking after her so well.

Danny was aware he was only useful as a driver for Spider. That is why Spider kept him close. Spider sensed that Danny was keen to make a break, as he had had enough of all the drama that Spider created. Danny was from the southern suburbs and had relations in the big city that Spider did not how of, so he was planning to move down to them, as soon as he got an opportunity, to get away from Spider. Danny and Spider returned to Emerald as it was impossible to run the drug supply from Eden, it did not make any sense. They took up residence with Mrs. Mathews again. Spider had boarded with her, before he met Danny, and he knew she was anti drugs. They were allotted one room on Spider's insistence, as he did not want Danny out of his sight. A few days later Spider got up early and went out to smoke some weed, thinking Danny was asleep. However Danny had been waiting for this opportunity and quickly got his things together and jumped into his car and left for the southern suburbs

Natalie was very excited when Jack told her he was the proud owner of the bakery in North Emerald, and she would have to show him more respect. She just laughed, and said she would now have to stay with him so she could spend all his money. The late nights were, no more, as Jack had to be in bed by 9 pm so he could be at work by 5 00 am. Natalie was not worried, as long as she had her Jack, she was happy. The fact that the Cantels now owned the bakery as well as the hotel and bar, was not to be advertised as it was considered a private matter, by the family. The bakery would still be called North Emerald Bakery so it would seem that Jack was employed there, and Olaf would not make folks any the wiser.

The first month was very hectic for Jack, as he tried to assimilate all the information. The process of warming the ovens up, how to mix the ingredients and for how long. Baking times, and how soon the products could be removed from the containers. Then the baking times differed for the buns, the bread and the pastries. But Jack approached the situation logically, he had a note book and all the relevant information went in there so he could go over it when he had time. The period from 5am. to 7am. was pretty hectic, as he was pushing to get some fresh bread on the shelves, for the customers, when they opened the door. After that the ovens were continuously supplying bread, buns, pies and pastries. Jack was quick to learn, and understand, the basic process of making the bread, so he felt more confident and happier. Now it was the pies and other pastries, which he wanted to understand, so as to put his stamp on them, with slight variations of the contents etc.

Once Tom and Eli were back from their honeymoon and in Tom's house they both relaxed. This was how it should be, no tension, no feeling of inadequacy, and no feeling of doing something that was not right according to the standards of society. Tom and Eli were now man and wife and they would be working towards the fulfilment of their dreams. Tom felt the best he had been in a long time, and was keen to reassess the planning for both businesses, the solar and the security. He felt more inclined, to increase production in the solar division, now that he felt comfortable in himself, about their situation. Brian could possibly cope with another installer without any drama. The two installers they had now were a competent team able to efficiently instal two systems in a good day. However they would not wish to be split up to teach new guys the job, as they would be put at a disadvantage. They had done the hard yards, they had no desire to repeat them. So Tom and Eli decided Brian should engage on person now, teach him how to prepare the panels, tubing, end caps, wiring and brackets in the workshop for the next job, then place them ready in containers for the installers to collect. Then start the process again with the requirements for the next job. In this way the workshop would be manned during working hours in case someone should turn up wishing to make enquiries about solar. Then the person could be given either Tom or Brian's mobile number.

Once they had run this scheme for a while they could reconsider the situation. Tom said he would discuss this with Brian and start doing it as soon as possible. In the case of Edwards Security things were a little more complicated. Tom had four installers, if he promoted his best installer, Craig, who was a licensed electrician, to chargehand and employed another installer, he could lighten his load at Edwards Security, and allow him to spend more time with Emerald Solar which he was hoping to expand further down the track. They agreed this was probably the best solution at the moment, so they would put it into effect. Tom felt sure Craig, his most competent installer, had the natural ability to be able to oversee, and help four installers in his care. He would source a new installer through word of mouth. All installers were electricians but not necessarily licensed.

Gerry thought that Spider and Shane Reynolds might be known to one another. He did not know Spider's origin, but apparently he had left home at ten or there about as he could not tolerate the hassle, for refusing to comply with his mother's demands. Whether this was in the city or elsewhere was unknown. Since then he had slowly degenerated into the thug that he now was. Not willing to listen or comply with any command if he did not feel obliged to do so. The police were virtually the only ones, that could force Spider to comply. Gerry felt that regardless of what was known or thought about the circumstances of Shirley's murder, there was no chance that Spider would ever admit to killing her, as he knew this would mean the end of his freedom. The biggest problem would be proving Spider had the handgun, and that he shot Shirley. Furthermore there had been no witness found to date, who could substantiate Spider's involvement.

Now that Tom and Eli were settled in at Tom's house they made a point of inviting Don around if they were having a barbecue on the weekends, Don was lonely and they liked to have him around and cheer him up a little. He seemed to get on well with Honey, Eli's Golden Labrador, and would be seen patting her or throwing a ball for her. It would seem they were good for each other. Don was very pleased, that Tom and Eli were now married, and he could see how well they were suited to one another. He felt Shirley would be very happy to see this. Tom would go and fetch Don and take him home when he wished to go.

TWENTY-ONE

Brian had employed one fellow at the factory, to work from the job drawing, he would cut the aluminium square tubing to length and attach all the end caps, then place the finished aluminium pieces along with the fittings, for the two installers to access, when they were ready for it. This had an advantage that there would be someone on the premises, at Emerald Solar during working hours. In addition they could train him to stand in, if one of the installers was sick. They would tell Brian to put the word out for two more able bodied guys to join their team. They would start off in the factory, learning how to prepare the parts for a job, put them in boxes ready to be taken by the installers.

At present Eli's coffee and sandwich shop would continue, under her very efficient management. Should Eli become pregnant, then there would be a review of the position with regards to Eli's health.

However they agreed that, if they had children, both of them working was not conducive to a happy marriage. Tom and Eli both loved children so they hoped they would be blessed by falling pregnant as time went on.

Jack was making steady progress, in his quest to understand, all the different things he needed to control, in order to be a successful baker. It was now two and a half months since Jack started at the bakery and Olaf was impressed with the way Jack had learned the various methods of making bread. Jack's success, could be put down to the way he had approached the task, keeping detailed notes of how to go about, the starting of the ovens, getting the big mixer primed and mixing the ingredients in correct proportions to start the day. Up till 7am it was busy and very hot, but once the bread started coming out of the ovens things began to move. The doors were opened and customers started coming in for fresh, hot bread. Jack did not believe in plastic bags for the bread, he put each loaf in a brown paper bag for the customer. This immediately showed the customer he was interested in supplying the best product he could. The same was to happen with the pastries, they were all placed in brown paper bags. The customers could get a loaf of bread sliced or whole, depending on their needs. Jack wished to make a few varieties of pies, and he discussed this first with Olaf and then with his mum and his sister Michele, and once he had the process under control, he started making his own style of pies, curry, chicken, beef and mince. Olaf could see Jack was behaving differently lately and asked, "Jack what is on the go"? Jack said "he had met the most beautiful girl, so he needed to learn the bakery business very well so he could marry her." Olaf chuckled "so you are in love, if that spurs you on, that is wonderful".

Sergeant Lowe and Sergeant Lewis decided to get Spider in for a chat, and see if they could make any headway. Spider turned up for this interview at the appointed time, and they let him wait as they had done to Rodney. However Spider's demeanour showed he was quite indifferent to this wait, as he had experienced it on more than one occasion. On entering the interview room the two Sergeants noticed he was his surly self. They asked why he had left town in such a hurry and he replied that it had been planned for two weeks. As it was at the time of Shirley Edwards murder did he know anything about it or did he have anything to do with it? He replied in the negative, saying he did not have a handgun. They asked him if he knew Shirley

Edwards, and he said he had never met her. They saw that Spider had arrived on foot, so they inquired what had happened to his friend with the car, and he said that he had moved on. They stressed upon him that if he wished to stay in town, he would have to behave, or they would be on to him. He mumbled that he did not make trouble it was the other people getting at him. They said he could go but they would be watching him.

****

Meanwhile over in Tegwans' Nest, Oliver had returned from his stint as a crew member on a fishing trawler but he did not look particularly tanned, as one would expect. His problem now was how to supplement his unemployment benefits. So that he could reimburse his partner for the mortgage payments she had made on his behalf while he was away. She had paid his share of the mortgage repayments, while he was residing at Her Majesty's pleasure. Things were not looking too good. He did not feel like returning to weed cultivation, but he needed cash and there were no jobs in Tegwans' Nest. If he tried growing the weed in the forest in pots, then there was the chance his neighbours might nick them. Maybe he could just start again in a small way, on his property, just until something came up. He had no desire to go back to prison as his stay had been very traumatic. He had been picked on, and beaten up four or five times for the amusement of the other inmates. He hated the place, but he had to make some money. This time he would be more careful, keep a better lookout, and plan an escape route.

Four months into their marriage, Eli told Tom one morning at breakfast that she was pregnant. Tom was over the moon, this was the best thing that had happened since their marriage. He was very concerned for Eli's welfare, and almost treated her like someone who was ill. She had to tell him she was expecting, not terminally ill, so he could treat her normally. He suggested she see her doctor to check all was well, and find out if she needed any supplements, as he was not taking any chances with this baby. Eli was delighted with his concern, and smiled at him in satisfaction, life was indeed good. Eli duly saw her doctor who was very happy with her condition, but did advise that Taekwondo, should really take a back seat, for the next 12 months. Then they could reassess the situation. Exercise classes for expectant mothers, was to be pursued to ensure she remained healthy and fit. Fortunately their house had four bedrooms, so they could prepare one of the unoccupied rooms, for their anticipated addition. Even if it was seven plus months away. Eli was extremely happy, not only was she married to the man she loved, but she was expecting his baby. They decided they would wait a month, before telling Gerry, Beverley and Neve. Meanwhile Eli started collecting things, that she would need for her baby.

Jack was doing very well at the bakery and Olaf told him so, which served to make Jack try harder. At seven in the morning he had the trays with the bread, pies and pastries ready for someone from their hotel, normally Michele, to collect. The next order was the other hotel on the north side. Followed by the order for "the coffee and sandwich bar" After that there was just a stream of customers coming for a loaf of bread or pies for lunch. The business was going well, and according to Olaf, Jack's sales were already better than his had been, prior to him selling the bakery. It was hard to know who was more excited, by the increase in sales, Jack or Olaf. The three months, that Olaf was to oversee Jack's purchase of the bakery was over. However Olaf was so used to turning up there every morning he could not stop himself, Besides he had nothing else to do, as his wife Greta had died five years back from cancer. Jack did not mind Olaf coming in, he was a good back up if Jack made a mistake, and they could chat. He told Jack stories about his time in Norway as a young fellow, and how he would go down to the docks as the trawlers came in with their catch. Back then the catch was usually very big, but in time it began to get smaller. His father had a bakery in a small town, Mandal, on the southern coast of Norway, it was here that he learned the art of making bread. The one thing that he disliked about Norway was the cold, it was not possible to escape it. So when he was 24, and Greta was 22, they decided to head south to the warmer climates.

TWENTY-TWO

They arrived in the big city after working their way south through Europe. Then working their passage on a steamer down to Capetown. There they had to find a ship going east and further down to the continent and the big city. Olaf said the city was too big for him so they travelled North, Arncliffe had a bakery so that would not do. So they went further North and ended up in Emerald where he started the bakery, and that was 45 years ago. Both of them were used to living near the sea, so they found Emerald to be an ideal place for them to settle. At that time there was no bakery in town so bread came from Eden, or people had to make their own. So when Olaf started the bakery he had customers ready to buy his bread, and this helped them to get established in the early years. So from that time on they never looked back. He knew the work was hard but he told Jack if he persevered, it would become easier as time went on. All of these conversations helped to motivate Jack, and deep inside he felt he would not let this opportunity escape him, he was in for the long haul. He knew he had no formal qualifications so he would have to create his niche in life, by hard work. If he wanted to be able to support Natalie, and any children they might have. The part he liked most of all was, what he produced was his own creation, and the folks seemed to like it.

At "George's Pub" life went on. During the week up until Fridays, Peter and George were able to accommodate the clientele. Come Fridays it became too busy, so they had engaged a girl who Michele knew, and she helped out, on Fridays, Saturdays, and on Sundays if required. The customers who came for lunches, really enjoyed Jack's pies, and they said so. Jack was a person who set himself goals, and once he was nearing that goal, he would set a new goal, so he would not struggle to keep going in the bakery. He found working alone was easy for him, he planned his day and just followed the plan.

The last payment on the hotel and pub was in a few days time and Chap had phoned to say he wished to meet George as usual. So on the evening of their meeting Chap was delighted to say to George the business was all his. They talked and reminisced about the ups and downs they had experienced getting to this stage, and George told Chap he was very grateful for the way he had helped them with finance, when they were going into a business, they knew nothing about. Chap replied the reason he did so, was he saw the determination in George's eyes, and he also knew that someone who had held a fishing license for 30 years must have great determination and drive, so he knew he had backed a winner. Now it was just the bakery to pay off but things were going well, and so far there were no concerns. Chap said they should continue to meet as there was still the bakery loan and George said he would like that.

Tom and Eli invited the Keane family, along with Don, around for a barbecue, one Saturday afternoon. Eli then announced to their friends that she was expecting a baby in about six months time. Gerry, Beverley, Jane and Don were delighted at the news and said they were sure, Tom and Eli would make wonderful parents. They were amused when they saw how Tom fussed around Eli making sure she did not do too much. Life for Eli, and Tom would be quite different from now on, with regular visits to the doctor, a visit to the gynaecologist and regular prenatal classes. Eli was just thrilled with the whole idea of having a baby, and Tom could not have been more attentive.

Natalie was progressing very well at work. Sometimes she was brought in to help Gerry's secretary in her office if her load was very heavy. When Gerry was dictating he spoke very quickly so the secretaries had to cope with a speed they were not comfortable with. For this reason they were continually starting, and stopping the Dictaphones so as to keep up with their boss. When Gerry had reached a decision, he needed it off his chest so he could deal with the next issue. The fact that his mind was so quick made it difficult for the girls, but they managed. He realised he was working at a very quick pace, but that was who he was. He did not do it out of malice, he would provide pastries from the bakery on occasion to show the girls he cared. Gerry could not change who he was, so he made allowances for the fact that it took them a while to catch up to him.

Jack closed the bakery at 4pm. and would quite often pick Natalie up from work. They would go to Natalie's home and Jack would produce meat pies, fresh bread and some pastries for an evening meal they would share with Mrs. Stokes. Who thought the world of Jack because of the way he treated Natalie and her. She thought that Jack was the best thing that had happened to Natalie. The evening walks that Jack and Natalie enjoyed around the lake were shorter now as Jack had to rise early in the morning to be at the bakery on time, but Natalie did not mind. She knew Jack was her man, and she would make allowances for the hours he needed to keep. Jack and Natalie were now very comfortable in each others company, and it was very reassuring. Hopefully they would be able to wed in the not too distant future.

****

One of the locals in Tegans' Nest, Sue aged 15, told her dad she would like a horse to ride. Her dad asked a friend who bred ponies if he would go along to the horse sales at Drummond to see if they could buy Sue a horse. Rex said he would go along and give them some advice. One Monday they drove all the way to Drummond to the sales there. There were plenty of spectators and buyers present. Coffee and hot dogs were being sold as some people had driven a long way, and required sustenance. Once the crowd were seated the horses were ridden in one by one, usually by the owner and he would proceed to show how capable his stead was. The buyers would bid as they saw fit, and usually the horse was sold. Many of these horses were for working with cattle so they waited until they were all finished. The horses for riding pleasure then appeared one at a time however they did not see one they liked until the last horse came in to the arena. It was a beautiful Palomino gelding, and Sue said she wanted it, so they entered the bidding process and acquired the horse. Sue was really over the moon. Rex arranged for one of the transporters to bring the horse over for them, and the horse was offloaded. Sue noticed that the temperament of the horse had changed since they patted him at the sale yards. Sue gave the horse some hay in the trough nearby, and then the horse became difficult to pat or put a halter on. When patting him Sue noticed a lump on his neck. The following day Sue and her dad had a hard time trying to catch the gelding, but eventually they did. It was clear this horse was not about to be ridden by a novice. Eventually they got hold of a local horseman who came over to look at the Palomino, and he said the horse had not been broken in. After further discussions, they told him about the lump they had found on the horse's neck.

He said unfortunately, that was a practise some people employed, tranquilize the horse until it has been sold. The horseman bought the horse off Sue at a reduced price and said he would try to break him in. Buyer beware!

Jack was getting more and more proficient in the art of producing top class breads, pies and pastries. To date he had made a dark bread, with a coarser texture and covered in poppy seed, and this was received very favourably by some of the public. So he knew he could make this, in limited quantities. His white and brown bread, including rye bread were very popular so these were made in larger quantities. The meat pies were available with chicken, beef, curried beef and beef mince filling, these all had a committed following by sections of the public. Pastries sold very well, as Jack reduced the pastry and increased the filling. All in all things were going very well. Olaf was impressed by Jack's motivation and open mindedness, with regard to his job and told him he was doing very well. Olaf could not help himself, most days he turned up at the bakery and kept Jack company. Jack did not mind, he enjoyed talking to the old man and he learned more information about the bakery. This included tricks of the trade, that he otherwise might not have become aware of. Olaf had not been in the bread business for 45 years in a strange land without learning how to survive.

George and Peter were doing well, they had a young lass, Bobbie, to help out in the bar on the days when things got busy, usually Fridays and Saturdays. George had made it clear to the clientele, that she was to be treated with respect, and there was no place for smutty jokes, or distasteful remarks. Bobbie became a hit with her engaging smile and pleasant manner. Some patrons suggested she should be on full time. The business in the bar, and the hotel had improved significantly since there had been that disturbance at the other pub on the north side and it had stayed steady since. Chap still paid his regular visits, to see George. Quite frankly if they stopped George would be at a loss to know, who to discuss his different ideas with. He had come to appreciate and enjoy Chap's involvement. He found Chap's advice very sound and he relied on it when making his decisions, on monetary matters. Teresa and Michele had learned an enormous amount about how to treat customers and what to expect. Michele had been to 16 working forums on hotel administration in the big city. These had given them new insight on how to go about functioning more efficiently. From what she had grasped Michelle was able to give Teresa a good idea of all the different ideas introduced at these events. Michelle continued to attend the forums each year.

Danny Bell had returned to his old stomping grounds and met up with some friends he had not seen in quite a while. These connections were instrumental, in getting Danny back into the work force. He was very grateful for the help, his friends provided him, to find a job. Danny was a simple fellow with an I.Q. of about 90, but he had some very good attributes. He was loyal, he carried no animosity, he would be at work every day, and do his job, without question, and he did not tell lies. However Danny was still traumatised by all the horrible things he was exposed to while associating with Spider. He did not realise, that he was tainted by what he had been forced to go through. He just felt very restless, uncomfortable and maybe a bit dirty. However he was able to find solace in his old surroundings and among his friends. Hopefully time would be the healer. Danny would be a good witness in court, but the police in Emerald did not know where he had disappeared to. The Emerald Police only realised he was gone when Spider turned up for his interview on foot. Spider claimed he had no idea where he was, but would like to have a word with him. Danny still had nightmares about his time with Spider. He was a passive and peaceful person. When Spider attached himself to Danny, he seemed incapable of breaking free. He was pleased he had taken the steps to get away from Spider, as Danny thought him a very bad person. Danny's mum still lived in the same house he had been born in. She was getting on in years and was delighted to see her Danny. His father had passed away from pneumoconiosis, due to working in the mines, for years. Danny stayed with his mum for a few days, and then said he had found boarding near his mates so he was off. Danny would be okay in his surroundings as he was quite well known.

Eli was now eight months pregnant, and looking and feeling great. In the early months of the pregnancy she had suffered from some morning sickness but this did not last. Now she had the baby's room ready with a white cot, a chest of drawers, a table for changing the baby's clothes and plenty of outfits. Tom and Eli had decided they would not enquire about the baby's sex, but would wait and enjoy the surprise on the day. Eli's gynaecologist was happy that all was well with Eli, and the birth could proceed normally. As long as the baby was healthy, that was the most important issue. Eli had taken maternity leave from her business, and left her trusted friend Barbara Wells in charge. Tom and Eli had discussed the options with regard to Eli's Coffee and Sandwich Bar, and decided to wait until the baby arrived before making any changes to the situation. Barbara had said, that if Eli wished to sell the business she would be interested in buying it. The purchase of a pram and stroller was left on hold until the baby was born so that they would know whether to buy blue or pink.

TWENTY-THREE

Spider was irate. As most people had things they wanted to do, he was able to hitch a lift from A to B and then he was on his own. How could people be so inconsiderate. Danny had been very self centred, leaving Spider in the lurch. He was livid about it, and if he ever saw him again he would let him know exactly how he felt. The fact was Danny had not deserted Spider, he had escaped from his grasp. Spider did not own Danny, in fact he had no right to enforce Danny to drive him around. He never liked Eden, moving there it was just a necessity, while the heat was on. Spider did not see himself being setup for Shirley's murder because the cops were too lazy to do their job. The incident of Shirley's death should have blown over by now and life should be able to proceed. This was Spider's first mistake. The people concerned had not forgotten about Shirley's brutal murder and they were still seeking a solution and conviction. Spider returned to Emerald thinking all would be quiet and peaceful again. So he could carry on his weed trade as before. This was Spider's second mistake. The police were getting more and more desperate and he might just be in the firing line.

Gerry, when he heard Spider was back in town, was certain this would have a detrimental effect on Rodney, and Gerry was right. Rodney seemed jumpy now that Spider was in town, and he wondered how long it would be before Spider and he crossed paths. Gerry suggested to George that he let Spider continue using "George's Pub" as his watering hole, as that way, they could keep some sort of eye on his movements. If he did not step out of line they might learn something. They were both surprised to see that Danny Bell was no longer Spider's driver, and they wondered where he had got to. George said that at the first sign of trouble with Spider he would be banned permanently.

****

It was now some considerable time since Oliver had come home from his stint in jail. He had managed through diligent cultivation of the weed to stabilise his financial position. He still felt aggrieved about being arrested by the police for cultivating the weed as it had set him back quite, considerably. He wondered who had given the police a tip off. Now he had increased his production by 100% to 96 plants. He vowed he would never go back to prison. During his time inside he had been beaten repeatedly, abused and called all the names under the sun. He had no idea why, it was just something about him, a portion of the inmates disliked. They needed no excuse to set on him, and once down they would put the boot in.

So as these things happen, the local police decided to pay Oliver a visit and see how things were getting along. According to all the information they had gathered Oliver was not working. They arrived in two unmarked cars, but Oliver was nowhere to be seen. So they walked around and counted 96 pots with marijuana plants in them, at various stages of growth. They decided to wait for Oliver as he could not be far away. Oliver had been out checking on his mud crab pots around the edge of the lake and collecting the crabs that had been snared. As he returned to his property he could see in the distance, two cars up near the homestead. This could not be a social call, he was not expecting any visitors. It must be the police, so Oliver did a U-turn and accelerated away. The police keeping watch from the house saw Oliver's manoeuvre and, quickly got into their cars to give chase. After about a kilometre of dirt road they were on the sealed surface so the police increased their speed. They soon started to close the gap between their cars and Oliver's ute. In five kilometres the police were on Oliver's tail. Realising that he was caught Oliver did the only thing he could think of. He turned the steering wheel abruptly, sending his ute careering off the road into a maize fields at high speed. Now a maize field is not level, it has small mounds and troughs in between the mounds. Because of the speed involved, the pickup travelled through the maize like a bucking horse hitting the mounds, becoming airborne and coming down it might hit a mound sending it up again, for 60 metres carving a pathway, before coming to rest.

The police stopped on the side of the road, and proceeded on foot to the wrecked ute. The sight was horrific. The pickup vehicle was completely wrecked from it's passage through the maize. The driver's door was open and Oliver was half in and half out of the vehicle. There was blood everywhere. He must have been travelling without a seatbelt, as he had head wounds that were bleeding profusely.

It appeared Oliver had been thrown around inside the vehicle. He had sustained some factures to his hands and arms making him look deformed. The vehicle was a complete right off.

An ambulance was called and a doctor but it was obvious to the police standing around this man was past help. His partner, when told, could not believe what she heard. She just stood in shock unable to speak. There would be a real storm over this issue. This was a very sad, and avoidable event that had escalated out of control. The police operation had lacked planning and foresight. They were harshly criticised by the media, for their aggressive approach. Those in the business of growing the weed, were particularly vocal saying, the poor individual's life was only worth a few marijuana plants. There was an inquest and the coroner's findings were, "self inflicted death, attempting to avoid arrest.". This certainly did not placate some of the public, and they voiced their opinions loud and clear in the local newspaper for the next few months. As he had requested he was cremated. His meagre possessions, were given to his son who lived in the big city. The property was repossessed as his partner in the venture, could not meet the instalments. This was a very sobering event for all the local weed growers, Watch your back.

Eli's labour was fortunately quite short for a first child, and all went well. This might have been due to the fact that she was very fit. A beautiful baby boy, weighing 3.2 kilos arrived making a lot of noise. Both mother and son, were declared fit and well. Tom and Eli were very happy with the new arrival. It entered Tom's mind on hearing the young fellow crying, that from now on nights would be quite different. The maternity home that Eli was in at Emerald had a full time job, finding enough place for all the bouquets that arrived with good wishes. Tom was very excited about his son, and spent some time with Eli and the baby, until he was told Eli needed "nurse attention" so he should go, and return later. Tom phoned Gerry with the good news, and they met at "George's Pub" to wet the baby's head. Gerry got hold of Bev and Jane to tell them the good news, and they very excited about the new arrival, and wanted to know when they could visit.

Tom told them the staff suggested the following afternoon for a short visit. When Tom visited Eli next he noticed she was very tired. So he did not stay long he just asked what they would call the young fella. Eli suggested Tom should choose a name as she would choose the name of their daughter. This was really amusing for Tom, and he asked when she decided she was going to have a girl next. They considered a number of names, and then decided on Gary Don Edwards. Tom phoned Don with the good news, and he was very happy about the event. The following day, Tom picked up Don and brought him to the maternity home to see Eli and the baby. Don was happy to see young Gary and said both Eli and Gary looked very well, and he was honoured to have Gary named after him. Gerry, Bev and Jane were also there and expressed their delight at seeing the baby.

Back home again, this time with a rowdy addition, the first few days were pretty hectic, so Tom took a few days off work, to help get some sort of rhythm going, so that they were able to feel more comfortable with Gary. Once they had achieved a regular feeding pattern and regular diaper changes, things became more manageable. It became increasingly obvious to Tom that Eli was more than exhausted. So he decided wherever possible he would attend to young Gary, and Eli could breast feed him. One month later on a Saturday after Gary was christened, Tom and Eli had Don and the Keane family around for a barbecue to celebrate the new arrival. Everybody was thrilled with the little bundle of joy. Gary was content when his tummy was full, and he had a clean diaper. Eli was very happy, and at ease with her baby so this must have transmitted to the young fella, making him quite easy to care for. Tom took the guys from Edwards Security, and Emerald Solar down to "George's Pub" for a few drinks. The fellas appreciated Tom thinking of them, and it just helped to strengthen the bond between the boss, and the workers. Tom and Gerry had a night out at "George's Pub" with George, Jack and Peter, enjoying a couple of drinks with them.

Tom took it upon himself to make an appointment with the gynaecologist who had tended Eli just to get a clearer picture of the situation. He was amazed, when he tried to understand, the terrible trauma of birth; and the subsequent demands on the poor mother. He left with a feeling of shame, imagining all was okay. Eli would need plenty of rest, and help and it was up to him to provide it. Eli was well known in Emerald, as she had grown up there, so it was not long before, gifts for Gary, started arriving at the door. Eli was overcome by the kindness, and generosity of the community. When you take into account the number of people who grew to know her through her "Coffee and Sandwich bar" over the years, then it all made sense. Nevertheless it was comforting to know there were people out there wishing them well. For the first three months, Tom tried to spend more time at home than at work so as to allow Eli to recover from the ordeal of giving birth, and become accustomed to the new way of life. Slowly Eli got the hang of dealing with this bundle of joy that called all the shots. Tom was beginning to feel, there was a lot more to life than working. He would have to plan to make more time for the family.

Four months on, little Gary had a lot to say that nobody could understand, but he brought Eli and Tom enormous pleasure. They spoke about Eli's Coffee and Sandwich Bar, and came to the conclusion, that Eli did not see herself going back to work there, as her family was her top priority now. Eli was hoping to be able to have a baby girl in due course. So Eli would give Barbara Wells first option to take over the business if she wished to. Barbara was dead keen to buy the Coffee and Sandwich Bar, but needed some help to make up the purchase price. Eli suggested she go and see Gerry Keane as he might be able to contact a very reasonable lender.

TWENTY-FOUR

Gerry was able to arrange the loan for Barbara Wells through Chap at a good rate, and the sale was successfully concluded. Now Eli felt she could concentrate all her energy on her family. She was very happy at the way Tom had received the new arrival, and felt sure he would be a good father, as he spent considerable time with Gary. He also had no problem changing Gary's diaper and enjoyed giving him his bath. Tom made a point of being home from work in the afternoons, to attend to these events. Tom felt that he had waited so long to have a son, that he was going to enjoy as much time with him as possible. Since the changes Tom had made at Edward Security, Craig had really shown his worth. He listened to the installers, and treated them all the same, showing no bias towards any one individual. Tom felt sure he had made a good choice in Craig as chargehand, and was using him to lighten his own load.

At the Emerald Solar workshop all the changes had worked successfully so far, but Tom was not altogether happy. He felt they needed two teams installing the solar panels on the roofs. He discussed this idea with Brian to see how he felt about the extra load. Brian said that it would require an additional certified electrician, as he was doing the maximum he could do in a day. Tom was happy with this as he had faith in Brian. He enquired if Brian knew of anybody that might be up to the job. Brian said he knew of a good fellow that could do the job, he just needed to contact him and ask him to come and see Tom if he was interested. Gerard duly arrived for an interview, and Tom was happy with what he had to say. Tom called Brian in, and he was advised the two had worked together before, so Tom said "Great, you can work together again if Gerard is happy to work under Brian." Gerard was happy with the requirements of the job, and agreed to start the following Monday. Now Tom said to Brian he had better order enough material for 12 jobs, and check how long that would last. It might be good to diarize when next to order stock. This changed everything the guys would be installing, four units a day in good weather. That might stop someone else from trying to enter the market. It looked as if Tom had just pushed the programme, as hard as he could under present circumstances, and he hoped Brian would be happy with the result. He certainly did not want to lose Brian. He was born and raised in Emerald where his dad had been a diesel mechanic for the council.

****

There were three children in all, one boy and two girls. The family was a caring and loving unit with each individual given space to develop. The girls had married and moved off to bigger towns with their husbands. Brian had remained in Emerald, he liked the atmosphere, and enjoyed the surfing. He met Mary at school in their final year and started dating. During this time Brian went on to qualify as an electrician with excellent results. He had no trouble finding a good job, with the council. Prior to marriage Brian and Mary did not engage in sex, as it was against their beliefs. Now it was time to marry Mary and settle down. The wedding was a small affair, just the two families and a small gathering at Mary's home. Brian and Mary went up the coast to a small resort for their honeymoon. While there, on the third morning after having woken up, lying in bed with Mary, Brian started initiating sex and Mary stopped him, saying, "but you had it yesterday". Brian was so taken aback he just swallowed hard, and said nothing. He was totally frozen, surely he had not heard correctly. Mary got up and went into the bathroom, and he could hear the shower water flowing. Brian slowly got up, dressed, and went out for a walk. How could this possibly be happening to him? Mary was loving and affectionate during their dating time together. There had never been any indication, that she was not keen on sex. That was not what just happened, Mary had just succeeded in switching Brian off,---permanently. What had he got himself into? Apart from being completely deflated, insulted, humiliated and devastated he did not quite understand. What was wrong with expecting sex two days running, after all were they not on honeymoon. Brian walked, and walked trying to decipher the demeaning message, he had just received, his world was upside down. Had he done something unacceptable, or had he been rough with Mary? He did not believe this as at no time, did Mary say anything was unpleasant. Apart from the absolute shock at hearing those words, never before in his life had he felt this crushed. He felt as if his feeling had just evaporated. Brian felt very deeply hurt and offended, his inside felt completely numb. He, in a short two weeks, had just learnt that women knew, just how to crush you. Brian's view of women took a turn at this time. He started to believe that, what women said had little to do, with what they thought or felt, it was mostly facade, and his trust in the female sex had suffered a body blow. He made no further attempt to engage in sex, while on honeymoon, as that had ended on day three. They came back to Emerald and moved into a council flat which suited them fine. Brian worked at the council and Mary was a secretary at a manufacturing plant.

Shortly after this Brian, heard about Tom looking for a good licensed electrician so he applied for, and got the job. Since then he was very happy working for Tom. However he never recovered from the honeymoon incident, he became a walking shadow of himself, as a man. He found solace in his work, because he was very good at it. He looked forward to work each day and was not really interested in going home to someone who was apparently frigid. He tried to behave normally, but would not introduce sex, no matter what. Mary for her part wanted to be intimate occasionally, and would make a move and Brian would pretend to respond, with no success. Under normal circumstances, this would have been absolutely devastating for Brian, but there was nothing normal right now, Mary had frozen his manhood. How much worse could it get?

So Brian carried on with this bizarre marriage for over a year until he decided he would make the break with Mary as the marriage was dead, Brian told Mary one evening that he wanted a divorce, her response was "just claim incompatibility". So he saw a solicitor, explained the situation and asked him to instigate divorce proceedings. The solicitor explained it was a process which would take three months but he felt sure it would be successful. In less than two years Brian was single again. Brian's feelings gradually softened towards women over time. He began to feel the need to explore the possibilities of finding someone more affectionate than Mary. Surely there must be some lady out there looking for love?

One day making an enquiry for Tom, at the council offices he met a very attractive, young lady Annette who worked at the reception. He found himself looking for an excuse to go to the council reception just so that he could see and talk to Annette again. After his third feeble excuse for turning up at Annette's desk, he asked her out for a drink, and she said sure.

Having been badly hurt once, Brian was extra careful with Annette. He knew he was very keen on her, and she seemed to be interested in him, but you never know. He decided he would take his time, and find out all the things Annette liked and disliked before he got too excited about her. Heaven knows he did not want to make a second mistake. Brian decided he would be up front about his situation. So sitting in the lounge of the local club enjoying a drink he told Annette about his marriage to Mary. How it turned out to be a disaster, and how, after months of this farce told Mary he wanted a divorce and she did not contest it. He was looking for a warm loving lady to share his life with, and he had no evil designs on Annette. He would treat her with respect, and should their feelings develop into something deeper, then they could see what they were prepared to do. Slowly this attraction between Brian and Annette became, something more serious.

Annette was divorced. Her ex, was a deep sea fisherman and he enjoyed fishing more than married life, so they had parted ways. Annette lived in a flat in north Emerald, and Brian started visiting Annette there. They would go out to dine or bring in a take away, and have a really good time together, chatting about their likes and dislikes or watching a movie. They always had something to do, and enjoy together. Eleven months into their courtship, after a lovely evening with Annette. Brian said he should be heading back to his flat. Annette said she was okay, with him staying over if he liked. Brian said he respected Annette, and was very fond of her, but he did not feel it was right for him to sleep with her before marrying her. Annette was not slow to reply, "Are you asking me to marry you?" to which Brian said "Oh,-- I guess I am". Well that was kind of sudden but it did reflect how Brian felt about Annette. She was not at all put out by this and said "Yes" in a loud voice, and jumped into his arms. All of a sudden Annette and Brian had set their future together, in motion. Brian still went home that night, but it did start them planning for their tomorrows.

The next few weeks flew by as they made arrangements for their wedding. It was decided that they would marry at the registry offices in Emerald. In light of the way Tom had treated Brian he approached Tom, and asked him to be a witness at the ceremony. Tom gladly accepted the invitation. The couple were duly married, and decided to get on with life, and have time away at a future date.

What they did do was, get each other a wedding ring, to seal their commitment to each other. They had some living to catch up on. Brian moved into the flat with Annette as it was more practical for them at this time. After a month of married life Brian took Annette in his arms one evening and said, "This is what I expected married life to be like.". Annette was very, very happy. Brian was very relieved to find that his performance sexually was back to normal, thanks to Annette's encouragement. He had been worried that the damage caused by Mary, might have been of a more permanent nature. Brian and Annette agreed they would hold no secrets, from each other so as to limit the possibility of stupid arguments. Back at work the guys were keen to go along for a beer with Brian and Tom to celebrate his marriage.

The landscape in Emerald was starting to change, a new pusher had been seen on the streets. It did not take long for this to come to Spider's attention, and it did not please him at all. He demanded, that Basil (his new driver) tell him who this new dealer was. All Basil could say was that he heard his name was Dart, but he had no further information. Spider got in the car and told Basil to do the rounds, so they could learn more about Dart. All Spider's runners had heard of Dart, some thought he came from the big city, other said he came from Arncliffe, but nobody was sure. Spider enquired when this Dart did his rounds. The runners all said it was usually about half an hour before Spider. So Spider decided he would meet Dart on one of his rounds.

One Sunday evening George gathered the family around saying there were issues they needed to discuss. Now that the bakery was running smoothly thanks to Jack's hard work, things needed to be reassessed. Jack would own the bakery, outright as he had proven himself over the time he had taken over from Olaf. However this did not mean that Peter and Michelle would lose out, on the contrary they were a very important part of the setup. George said that Jack had spoken to him, about he and Natalie getting engaged, then married in the new year, and this had his blessing. Peter, Teresa and Michelle were very much in favour of this as they could see they were well suited to each other. As far as Peter and Michelle were concerned. Their share had increased proportionately as the business increased in value. George and Estelle were hoping Michelle and Peter would stay on in the partnership as they were well acquainted with the workings of the business and their shares would continue to grow. However if one left now the strain it would place on the remaining three would be substantial. Both Michelle and Peter said they were happy to stay for the foreseeable future. George pointed out that Jack still had some share in the hotel and pub, as the bakery did not cover all his worth. So in the future at sometime they would decide how to recompense him and Natalie.

Now this issue of Dart, needed some planning. Most of the runners were stationed on open road, where they could just step out of a door way. However towards the industrial area there was one spot where the pusher would need to turn in between two buildings off the road and the only way back, to the road was by reversing back onto it. Spider decided Dart would be dealt with there. On the day, Spider and his driver, Basil were in their car, parked across the road from the site in a garage access, back a little from the roadway. Basil was to drive in behind Dart, as he turned in between the buildings. One of Spider's runners was to give a signal, as they saw Dart's car coming down the road. At the appropriate moment Spider was given the signal, and as Dart's car drove up between the two buildings, Basil crossed the road, and drove in behind Dart restricting his exit.

All hell broke loose, before Dart realised what was happening. Spider had opened the driver's door and pulled Dart from the vehicle. There was a mad flurry of fists, mostly Spider's and Dart lay on the ground. Spider spared nothing, he kicked and bashed Dart until he was just an unrecognisable human. He then bent down to Dart and said "if you ever come back here, I will hurt you". Spider jumped back into Basil's car, and they sped off. In three minutes, there was only a very badly beaten Dart lying in the dirt. Somebody contacted the ambulance and they turned up, horrified at what they saw. They did what they could for the poor fellow, and after the police were finished with their initial enquiries, they took the man to hospital in Eden.

The hospital staff in Eden were very upset, that one human being, could do this to another one of his own species. Dart suffered, a broken jaw, a broken eye socket, three broken ribs, a possible broken arm (subject to x ray) and severe bruising to his torso, arms and legs. He would be in hospital for some time. The local police were not the idiots Spider thought they were, they recognised the work of Spider when they saw it. Early next morning Sgt. Lewis was already busy putting out feelers to try and get some feedback on this terrible assault. It did not take long for a snitch to say "This guy was on Spider's patch." Sgt. Lewis lacked the necessary witnesses to put Spider inside for a serious length of time, but he was hopeful something might come up.

TWENTY-FIVE

Two days later, an elderly lady arrived at the police station, and asked to speak to whoever is in charge of the assault on Bremmer Street (this being the street where the horrific assault took place). Sgt. Lewis was notified, and he came forward to speak to the lady (Mrs Lunt). He introduced himself, and asked how he might help the lady. Mrs. Lunt replied "I am here to help the police." Sgt. Lewis ushered her into an interview room, and arranged for Sgt. Bert Lowe to be present. They started the tape, and asked Mrs. Lunt to elaborate. She began by saying, "I am a resident on Bremmer Street, and on the day of the assault, I saw the whole event go down. My upstairs flat is over the road, from the open space where the first car parked. I happened to be upstairs sitting near the window to catch some of the warmth of the sun. When I heard a car pull up so I looked out of the window and saw a car off the roadway between the two buildings. Then, another car immediately pulled up behind the first car. A fellow got out of the passenger seat of the second car, ripped open the driver's door of the first vehicle, dragged the driver out, and proceeded to lay into his quarry something terrible. After which he jumped back into the car he came in, and rushed off." Realising the enormity of this statement Sgt. Lewis was quite concerned for Mrs. Lunt's safety. He asked Mrs. Lunt "do you have family or do you live alone." She replied "My husband died two years back and my children are married, and have moved away, so I live alone". When asked, she said "I do not know the assailant, but I feel sure I would be able to recognise him again."

Sgt. Lowe organised a series of a dozen mugshots of known offenders and showed them to Mrs. Lunt, asking her " please look through these photos, and see if you can recognise the offender among them." It took Mrs. Lunt less than a minute to draw their attention to Spider Kelly. They asked her if she knew who the person was, and she said "I have no idea. However I am sure he is the person guilty of the assault." This was excellent from the point of verification, but it posed a problem now. If Spider heard about her, she would disappear off the face of the earth. The police desperately needed a conviction against Spider, they needed to curb his rampage. Spider believed he could not, be held responsible for Dart's assault, as all the witnesses were his guys, so there could be no witness. Spider was picked up without any trouble and brought in for interview. He was as cocky as ever saying he knew nothing about any assault on the day concerned, and he would like to go.

He was duly charged, his mobile, and belongings were taken from him, and he was allowed a phone call to his solicitor. Then he was shown the inside of one of the cells. Later that day Spider's solicitor, Cyril Thiems arrived, and the interview was conducted. Sgt. Lowe said that Spider was accused of assaulting an individual, Dart, in Bremmer Street, Emerald at approximately 4.45 pm. three days previously, on Monday the 16th of May. Spider denied this, saying it was ridiculous. He and his mates were playing footy on Nine Mile Beach at that time. The police countered that, there was an eye witness to the sordid affair. Spider shouted, "that's impossible there was nobody there". This statement was recorded, and Spider tried to say he had made a mistake, but it was too late. His response had been noted. Sgt. Lowe told Solicitor Thiems, that

Spider would be held over until his arraignment, and subsequent trial. This was met with plenty of bad language by the accused in spite of his solicitor trying to keep him quiet. Spider was led away to the holding cells.

Sgt. Lowe was concerned about Spider's accomplices getting to Mrs. Lunt, so he was hoping they could move her to a safe place until the trial. He discussed his concerns with Sgt. Lewis who appreciated the way these thugs operated on fear, as a deterrent. They decided to speak to the public prosecutor in this regard, and he agreed with the idea of protecting Mrs. Lunt. He pointed out that he was very eager to get this case to court as the chances of sending Spider down for a while were excellent. The case came before Judge Mason on the following Monday, and he set the case for trial two weeks later. The defence tried to say that was too soon, but the judge said the defendant claimed there were no witnesses, so it would not be a problem, to arrange a defence. Spider's plea for bail was rejected outright.

Meanwhile the prosecution had a few hurdles to negotiate. The public prosecutor had a meeting with the judge discussing all the possible ways Spider would try to get to Mrs. Lunt and, they decided they would not put Mrs. Lunt's life in jeopardy. Mrs.

Lunt was to make a sworn declaration in front of the judge with regard to what she saw, and when she saw it and she would not be present in court. The prosecutor found out that Mrs. Lunt had a good friend living in Arncliffe, whom she had not seen for some time. So arrangements were put in place for Mrs. Lunt to visit her friend for a month. As soon as her statement was completed she could gather the requirements for her stay in Arncliffe and she would be transported there in an unmarked police car.

On the 30th day of May the trial of Spider Kelly got underway with Judge Mason presiding. The court was packed, with the public keen to see what was going to happen in the Spider assault case. The trial was short, and to the point. Judge Mason heard the prosecutions case. The doctor who attended Dart at the site, told the judge of all the injuries, Dart had sustained, and that he would be in hospital for some time. The defence tried to say, that Spider and his mates were playing soccer on Nine Mile Beach, at the time in question. The prosecutor then informed the defence there that there had been an eye witness, and again Spider blurted out "there was no one there ". The sworn declaration of the unnamed eye witness, was read out to the court, and accepted as evidence.(The name of the witness appeared on the court documents but was suppressed, to avoid Spider trying to retaliate against her.)

The judge in summing up said to Spider, "it was extremely doubtful if you would recognise the truth if you saw it. You live by violence and outright intimidation. You will be required to undergo various workshops, in prison, in an effort, to try to rehabilitate you. The results of which, will depend on your attitude, towards changes for the better." Judge Mason further said that, "the only way to approach this case, was to take into account all his previous misdemeanours. Making sure that the sentence would be of sufficient duration, to allow Spider time, to make the necessary adjustments, before being allowed back into society."

Judge Mason sentenced Spider Kelly to four years in jail to be served without any option of an early release. The Judge ordered the Constable to take Spider Kelly down.

One morning when Tom arrived at the Solar Shop he saw Brian grinning at him and asked what was up. Brian replied that Annette was expecting their first child. Tom, grinning, congratulated Brian and asked, if all was well. Brian said Annette had seen the doctor twice so far and everything was good. The doctor gave her a list of suggested exercises, she should try to do to help keep her body in good shape for the birth. Brian said the baby was due, in five months. Tom said they would have to wet the baby's head together. Brian went on to say the deliveries from the big city, were not as regular as they hoped, so he would need to put in another order to prevent them running out of parts. Tom said if they had to, that was fine. They could not afford to run out of parts and have the men standing around waiting to finish a job. There was place in the workshop they could set aside for supplies.

TWENTY-SIX

Sergeants, Lowe and Lewis were very pleased with the sentencing as they felt jail was the safest place for Spider, away from society. However they still had one thing to do, and that was search Spider's digs. The public of Emerald were quite relieved when they heard the outcome of the case, they felt free and at ease. Sgt. Lowe made contact with the prison services at the prison Spider would be confined to, asking that Spider be put in with a snitch, to see what info they could glean from the association. The search of Spider's room, at Mrs. Mathews boarding house, produced some marijuana, a short sword, and an eight inch knife. Sgt. Lowe expected more, they must have missed something. They would have to do another search.

Both Tom and Gerry were very pleased with the sentence given to Spider, and looked forward to a period of some peaceful existence. As a matter of fact everybody in Emerald heaved a sigh of relief with the news of Spider's internment. Life was good again. Little Gary was thriving and making plenty of noise, but Eli was in her element, enjoying every minute of the day with her young son, who was showing some red hair. Tom enjoyed time with Gary daily, when he got home from work, and was looking forward to the day, he would be able to play with him out on the front lawn. Tom felt very blessed, he had been through terrible trauma and grief with Eli but a new dawn was bringing them, great happiness. Gerry experienced much pleasure, when he watched Tom with Eli and Gary, and he was very happy that life, had turned around for them. His one big aggravation was that the culprit for Shirley's horrific murder was still at large. Gerry was a very resilient man, he had not given up, nor would he.

Jack and Natalie were getting on very well and were unofficially engaged. Natalie had no engagement ring but she was happy to sacrifice that to bring the wedding forward. Jack, through his hard work had improved the sales figures, for the bakery since he first took over. This was largely due to his efforts, to accommodate the customers. He made five different loaves of bread, a number of rolls and buns, and all sorts of pastries. He was testing the market, those that did not sell would be removed, from the production list. Jack worked long hard hours 5am - 4pm that was a long day. Saturdays from 5am -noon. Sundays he spent with his wife to be. They were always discussing plans for their future, and this was good. It is quite normal to have some idea of, where you are going. Jack told his father, that he and Natalie wished to marry. They would forgo the engagement to save money, and they were hoping the wedding could be held at the hotel. George was delighted, with the idea. Teresa, Michelle and Peter were all keen on the idea, and wanted to know when. They held a meeting, with Natalie present, so they could iron out any problems.

It seemed a Sunday would be the most convenient day as the bakery was closed. They thought in three months time they would be ready to tie the knot. Jack said he had asked Olaf if he could run the bakery for two weeks and he was happy to do so. The hotel was in the shape of a U for a reason. Halfway down each side of the U there were folding doors that could be drawn to the centre from each side, and there was extended roof covering to this area. Thus creating a suitable enclosed space for an occasion like a wedding. Tables and chairs would be placed on the carpeted area leaving enough space for people to dance on the wooden floor. This still left a large beer garden area for patrons to enjoy outside. As the bakery would be closed, all preparations would need to be made in the hotel kitchen, but this would be easily done, as there were many hands that could be put to good use. Michelle would be in charge of decorations, flowers, balloons, streamers etc. Teresa felt confident the staff would manage the event successfully. There would be a main table for the bride and groom, George, Teresa, Mrs. Stokes Peter the best man and Olaf. It was hoped the other guests would mix, as they sat around the other tables. Jane had been asked if she would kindly play the wedding waltz, "Dear Heart "on her violin. Michelle said she had a casual, who could help turn out some lovely pastries and other eats for the event which would be buffet style. The idea was to make it casual with all the guests mixing. The hotel chef, and staff would provide the many different cuts of meat. Guests would include:-

Mrs. Stokes; the Keane family; the Edward family; some of Natalie's friends from work; Olaf; Peter and partner a few of Jack and Peter's friends, in all about 30. The couple did not want a big wedding, just the people that meant something to them.

The young couple had discussed the situation of them living with Mrs. Stokes, and she was very happy about it, as she would have more company. This situation was to be temporary, and they would see how it worked out. Mrs. Stokes could not be left alone 24/7, she was confined to her wheelchair because of arthritis, and was in pain more often than not. While the newly weds were on honeymoon, they had convinced Mrs Stokes to stay at the hotel, along with her canary, so Teresa and Michelle would be able to help her. As time went on Jack and Natalie would make adjustments as necessary. The Cantel family was very pleased with the idea of Jack and Natalie getting married, there was excitement in the air, and now Peter was dating a young lady, Lesley Morrow who lived with her parents and brothers. They ran a fuel outlet, as well as a service and repair shop, on the south side of Emerald. The family had been in Emerald for many years, the parents having grown up, and attended school in Emerald. They were well known as good, honest people, a credit to the community.

Gerry phoned Tom, with some good news. A property was about to come on the market soon, and Gerry believed it had potential, could Tom meet him after work at "George's Pub"? Tom said he could, and made plans with Eli to expect him a little late. Gerry was already sitting in the private bar, awaiting Tom's arrival, this must be good! Tom sat down, and they ordered beers, then Gerry unrolled a map of North Emerald, which must have been 40 years old. Tom could work out where the main road North was, and where Gerry's offices would be now. Gerry pointed further north to Murray Street. Now Murray Street joined Peterson Place and Shepherd Rest the other side, towards Nine Mile Beach, was without name. The point was this block of land had not been on the market before. It had been part of a dairy farm, way back in time. It was just over five hectare in size, had a couple of old houses on it which were very rundown. It was partly fenced and was an eyesore, to the town folk. The owner, an old man of 90, had passed away recently, and it would be coming up for mention on the notice board at the courthouse in one or two days. In instances of this nature, where the estate has to be settled expeditiously, as there were no remaining relations, the courts disposed of the assets speedily to wind up the estate. There was no need to secure top price for all the assets. So as the items appeared on the list of assets they were advertised on the court notice board and the first offer would be accepted. Any other approach would delay the process of settling the estate, costing the courts and taking up extra time. He had been the last remaining member of the family, that owned the dairy farm. However, it was essential they were ready and waiting, as it would be first come first serve, so as to facilitate the tedious task, of going through all the procedures.

Now there were two interesting things about this property. One, the solicitors for the family were old friends of Gerry's neighbour who had just mentioned in passing to Gerry, that it would be a bargain. When advertised at the law courts, it would be an unknown piece of land. If Gerry made an immediate offer, it would be accepted, as it needed to be disposed of, to wind up the estate. The second interesting point was, that the owner had the site rezoned for development, a few years before he got so sick. Therefore, they would be able to develop the site, with minimum fuss when they decided to. The idea Gerry had was, he and Tom could go in 50/50 and buy the land, as an investment, in time as things improved they could, either develop the property or resell it. Gerry was led to believe, if they offered eight or ten thousand dollars the land would be theirs.

Make no mistake, this was a good proposition. Tom was keen, so Gerry took him for a drive, past the location and the two agreed it had potential. Tom said he would like to run it by Eli first, and Gerry agreed. Tom went home and over the evening discussed the idea with Eli who said, "If we have the money, and Tom was of the opinion it was a good idea, then she was all for it." Tom contacted Gerry by text saying "all good, go for it". The next day Tom received a text from Gerry, "need $4500 plus signature". So Tom and Gerry became the owners of the "Dairy Land". Among the papers pertaining to the property was a very old map, which showed the area as it had been, 60 odd years before. The two old houses, one set towards the west side, and one to the north end, it appeared they might have had a vegetable garden, as not too far from one of the houses, there was a borehole indicated on the map. Although well built, the houses were very old, and had not been maintained for years. Tom and Gerry realised the old timber, was in good condition in many areas, and this would sell at a premium in today's world. They needed to get the fencing around the property attended to first, as it was dilapidated. They would also need to see about getting someone, to reclaim the good planks from the house, once the site was fenced.

After six weeks in hospital Dart, was released back into the dangerous world. He was walking with a limp, and his nose seemed to have a bend in it. He looked subdued, and went to a car waiting for him, and he was driven away, not to return to Emerald. From prison Spider managed to keep his business of supplying drugs going, but to a much more limited extent. On the Sunday morning following the purchase of the "Dairy Land", Gerry paid a visit to the property he and Tom had acquired, and went looking to see if he could find the borehole, he had read was on the site. After about 20 minutes of removing weeds and debris, Gerry saw it sticking out of the ground, by about 150mm. There was a loose cover over the pipe, which he removed. Running down into the borehole was a wire. Gerry took the wire carefully in his hands, and started raising whatever it was secreting. One metre of wire, finally brought up a parcel, wrapped in machine cloth, used to protect metal from rust, it being well covered in grease. Gerry checked nobody was in the vicinity, and carried the parcel to the nearest house. Here on the verandah, he slowly unwrapped the contents, which turned out to be none other than a 9 mm hand gun, complete with factory fitted silencer,-- WOW, what a find! Realising he would have to hand it in to the Police, or face serious consequences, he first phoned Tom, and asked him to come over. Tom not a lover of firearms, was stunned and horrified, when he saw the instrument of Shirley's death. Gerry consoled him by saying, if he had not called Tom, there would have been permanent feeling between the two of them, and there friendship might have suffered as a result. This friendship with Tom was very important to Gerry.

TWENTY-SEVEN

Together, Gerry and Tom took the firearm along with the packaging, down to the police station on the south side. As they had wrapped the gun up, in the packaging again, it was not apparent what it was. Det. Sgt. Lowe met them, and took them into an interview room, where he had the pleasure of unwrapping the weapon, and just about jumped with joy, he was so excited. He immediately called, Sgt. Lewis who came from home, to see the deadly weapon, they had been seeking for so long. Tom and Gerry had to explain, that they had bought the "Dairy Land" up at the North end of Emerald, and while looking around the property, they found the gun, hidden down a borehole. They were obliged to take the two Sergeants to the site, so they could write a report about the recovery, of this, most important piece of evidence. It was decided that, the only people who would know about this, in Emerald would be Tom and Gerry and the two Sergeants. Tom asked Gerry, not to say anything to Eli as it would torture her.

The handgun, would go straight to ballistics, so they could try to match it to the four 9mm bullets and casings recovered. Two from Shirley, and the two from the bikie, in the big city. Among the Emerald police, there was little doubt, it was the murder weapon, but the courts would require proof beyond doubt. The police in the big city, were not happy, that they had not found the firearm, but could do nothing about it, as all procedures had been followed. So the ballistic results would be forwarded, to both police stations when they became available. Meanwhile in Maloney Prison, Spider was not happy. He had been beaten up twice, for trying to exert some authority, over other inmates. Now life was not so good, as he was just a small cog, in a big wheel, and his opinion was of no consequence. He was obliged to attend classes, twice a day, except for Wednesdays, and produce a write up, of the previous days classes. Although Spider was street smart, he was not that familiar, with the inside of a classroom. All of this became very apparent, when Spider had to submit his report, on the previous day's work. There was, no summary, of the previous day's work, Spider was incapable of producing a report of the work, as he had no idea what they were talking about. The time inside, was going to be a good education for Spider.

As a small boy Spider had been a handful, for his mother. There were six children in all, and his father, was a construction worker, who came home one week in every four, so parental guidance was low down, on the list of priorities. Spider being the eldest, had a certain amount of say, in the household when Dad was away. He quickly learned how to skip school, and meet up with some of his mates down at the beach, where they avoided detection from authorities, by hiding in the sand dunes. In short time they started smoking cigarettes, and soon became addicted to nicotine. Being a bit street wise, it was not long before Spider at the age about 10 became a runner, and soon he was well known in the business. After eight years as a runner, he reckoned he could make more, if he ran his own little group, and from there it would just get bigger. If somebody crossed his path, he would beat the living daylights out of them and carry on.

Gerry was very happy, with the find of the weapon, and he felt there was a much better chance of linking the gun, to Spider now than there had been before. Gerry found out where Spider and Danny had been staying in Emerald, and went around there and spoke to old lady, who owned the house. He told her, he was keen to find Danny Bell, as he had some important information for him. The old lady, Mrs. Mathews, said she might have something for him, so off she went to have a look. She returned with a letter for Danny Bell, which she said she had received, quite a while back and showed it to Gerry. Gerry saw the address of the sender written on the back of the envelope, and it was in the southern suburb of the big city. Gerry said he really needed to contact Danny, would she mind if he took the letter with him, so he could further his inquiries. Mrs. Mathews said it was no good to her, and as long as he was going to Danny, he might as well take the letter with him. It might help to find Danny.

Gerry was in a quandary. He was trying to find the killer of Shirley, the wife of his good friend Tom, but he could not share all the information with him, as it would be too distressing for Tom. So Gerry did the only thing he could, he kept it to himself. Sharing the information he now had with the police, might not be the smartest thing to do, as they might charge in and cause Danny to disappear. So he would have to think up another idea, that would not entail the police, at this stage.

Before anybody realised it the wedding day had arrived. Teresa and Michelle had done a beautiful job of preparing the venue, with coloured ribbons, streamers, balloons and arrangements of flowers, it really was exquisite. The Area inside the U formation of the hotel was large, part was carpeted and the rest of the floor was wood. The main table was positioned to accommodate George, Teresa, Mrs. Stokes, the bride and groom, Peter, the best man, and Olaf. All the tables were arranged in an arc, along the carpeted floor. Chairs were placed in no specific order around the tables, with the idea of getting the friends to mix. Music would be provided by a small band of keyboard, drums and guitar. Jane Keane had agreed to play the bridal waltz, "Dear Heart" on her violin. The guests started arriving at 11am and the marriage celebrant arrived on cue to perform the ceremony in front of all. The bride in white, looked beautiful and big Jack looked quite dapper in a grey suit. They were a lovely couple, and the guests were vocal in their approval. George made a speech welcoming Mrs. Stokes and Natalie into the family, and raised a glass to the event. Peter was very nervous, when he had to say something, but pulled it off without any hiccups. Jack surprised many of the guests with his ability, to think on his feet thanking his parents, for all the help they had given Natalie and him. To Mrs. Stokes, a special warm thank you, for having such a lovely daughter. To the guests a thank you for coming, please enjoy the event. Jane produced a beautiful rendition of "Dear Heart" for the bridal waltz. The guests cheered, as the couple floated across the floor, and many people took photos of this wonderful event. Everybody had a lovely time chatting to other guests and partaking of the tasty eats provided. The guests thoroughly enjoyed the occasion, and many remarked on Jane's superb performance on the violin.

But alas, nothing lasts forever, soon it was time for the bridal couple to take their leave, so everybody gathered outside in the courtyard to cheer them off. They were to spend 10 days, up the coast at a private resort. After every exciting event, there is a sadness that descends, over those left behind and Mrs Stokes felt it most of all. So Michelle and Teresa did their best, to keep her mind busy on other matters. She had her own room with her canary, next to Michelle, so if she needed help in the night, she could press an aid button, that would alert Michelle.

Time had moved quickly, since the wedding and Gary Edward was turning one year old. His greatest interest, was in how big the cake would be, and if

Jane would be coming. Gary had developed an attachment, to Jane over the last few months, and given the chance he would follow here around the house. Eli was very proud of her Gary, and delighted at how well he could walk. Jane was quite delighted that Gary was so keen to be near her and she was fond of him. However Gary's biggest hero was his dad, Tom who would hoist Gary onto his shoulders and move around the garden. Today they would be having a barbecue as well as a cake, and Don, Gerry, Bev and Jane would be present.

Brian was impressing Tom, with the way he had everything at his fingertips, and this made a difference to his crew, as they knew Brian would be asking them, about the jobs they were on and what was next. Emerald Solar was beginning to hum. Brian was a changed man, since his marriage to Annette. Craig was carrying the load, very well at Edwards Security whenever Tom was busy working on quotes for big premises, or attending to other matters pertaining to the businesses. At present, there were three, big projects on the go, in the industrial sites in north Emerald, so Tom was having meetings with the owners, and working on quotes to secure the premises. The security, these days was very different to what it used to be. No more wires, laser beams were the way to go. Unseen by the human eye, they could be broken by someone and he would never know, until asked what he was doing there, by a police officer. So stacking, inside these structures, had to be very precise, so as to avoid breaking a laser beam.

The good news, about the handgun and the bullets, set Emerald Police Station abuzz. They were a perfect match. So now, it could be said with confidence that gun had been used, to shoot both Shirley, and the gang member in the city. The security police had been busy, in the interim pursuing inquiries, as to how this handgun, complete with silencer got into the country. Their findings, led them to a crane driver down at the docks, in the big city, who apparently had a contact on the docks, who arranged for the illegal import of special guns into the country. These guns were brought to the crane driver, and he smuggled them through customs, and sold them to interested parties. The lucrative, illegal imports had been going on for at least two years. The crane driver was arrested, and subsequently charged, for receiving illegal imports, and sentenced to six years in jail. Further investigations, failed to unearth the identity of the contact on the docks. One of the difficulties for the police in the city, was tying the handgun to a particular member of the gang, to be able to lay murder charges. It was not possible to charge the whole gang, as there would suddenly, be hundreds of alibis to say the members were elsewhere. With the extra information the city police had, about how the handgun arrived in the country, they were putting pressure on their informants.

Meanwhile in Emerald the police were very busy, working out, how Spider might have got hold of the gun. The police had noticed that since Spider's incarceration, Rodney did not seem scared any more. While this was going on, the informant (Ian) in the prison cell with Spider, had managed to rescue Spider, from a severe beating, again. He was in the hospital bay with Spider, explaining to the nurse, what had ensued. Spider was beginning to think, that maybe his cell mate was, okay. Spider was in the sick bay for three days, before he returned to his cell, complete with plenty of bruises. Ian asked Spider, how come the inmates were always laying into him, but Spider just said they were bastards. Spider continued going to his classes, each day, and he was learning to write and read properly. The word arrived in the jail, that the handgun had been found by the police, in Emerald. This was a blow to

Spider, the net was slowly beginning to close, but Spider did not think so. He and Ian were sitting in the cell talking one evening, about their lives and things they had done. Ian said he had beaten his wife so badly, she was in hospital for a month. Not to be outdone Spider said he had shot a lady, not once, but twice, and she died, but the cops could not prove it.

One could almost imagine, these beatings of Spider, and Ian's care of him, were engineered. Ian knew now, that his position was very unsafe. If Spider got an inkling, that he was a police informant, he would be dead. Luckily Ian's "Mum" would be coming to see him, on the next visiting day. Ian was anxious, he did not feel safe, but the day duly came around, and Ian was shown into the meeting room, with his "Mum" at the table. Ian greeted her, and sat down to talk to Snr. Sgt. Mabel Lincon. Trying to seem downcast, and unhappy, Ian told her all that had been said, between him and Spider Kelly. The next week, Ian was moved from that prison, to another district where, he would be required to face, further serious charges, Spider was shocked, he seemed like such a good guy.

The only problem with this evidence was it was all verbal. Yes you can say one, is a felon the other a police officer, that is perfectly correct, but Spider will say they were bragging, to see who could outdo the other. He did not have a gun to shoot anybody, and that would be stupid, as that would mean serious time. But Rodney was still around, so the police decided to put more pressure on him. He was told to report to the Emerald Police Station, to see Det. Sgt. Adam Poole at 9am on the following Monday morning. Rodney did not know any Det. Sgt. Poole so what could this be about? Everything was quiet with Spider in jail. Monday morning came and Rodney had to have something to give him some Dutch courage, so he went into the garage, and had a couple of good swigs, from the vodka bottle he kept there. He arrived at the police station on time and was led into an interview room, where he took a seat. This was so unfair, they went out of their way, to make Rodney anxious and nervous, but this time he only waited five minutes before Det. Sgt. Adam Poole arrived with Sgt. Fred Lewis. Fred introduced Rodney to Dec. Sgt. Poole, who was leading the inquiry into Shirley's death now. Adam told Rodney the gun used in the egregious slaying of Shirley, had been located in Emerald, so now there were many questions to answer. Why was it necessary to murder Shirley Edwards? Who had asked for the slaying?

What part did Rodney play, in this atrocious act? Did he realise, he was in very serious trouble with a possible prison sentence, hanging over his head? Poor Rodney, he could see bad times were coming. He tried desperately, to deny any involvement in the dastardly deed. Adam warned him that aiding and abetting was a very serious charge, as was, being an accessory after the fact. Adam further pointed out, Spider was in prison for a limited time, and then he would be out. Is that what Rodney wanted? The longer Rodney waited, to come clean the worse it would turn out to be. Now Rodney was in a bad way, and it was very plain to see. Adam said the best thing Rodney could do, was go away, think it over very carefully, and return with representation.

Rodney went straight to "George's Pub" where he ordered a double vodka and a beer, and went sit alone in a corner seat, where he would not have to talk to anyone. Rodney needed to think. If he told all that he knew, (the truth) then his future looked extremely bleak. If he denied any knowledge of the horrendous murder, then it could be very dangerous. He had absolutely no intention, of setting eyes on Spider ever again, he was pure hell on earth. Rodney would give himself a few days to think about it.

At last the city police got a break, squeezing the

crane driver real hard, they learned he had sold the handgun fitted with silencer to a member of a motorcycle gang, called Shane. He had a ponytail and was thickset. One of the police in the City, remembered that the last bikie to die was called Shane --- he could not remember the surname but he read it in the local newspaper. The police inquiry into the death of Shane Reynolds, had so far produced no information. The informants were not talking, it was probably too dangerous. However two detectives who attended the funeral, to see if they could learn something, noticed a lawyer there who they recognised, as Jim Cotter, who did represent bikies, on occasions. So after some smooth talking Jim told the police Shane Reynolds was the victim, of an ambush, down at the old police station in May street.

Well this was a start, if nothing else, so Shane Reynolds bought the handgun from the crane driver, and used it to assassinate a member of the Bulls motorcycle gang. This was all supposition but it was possible. Then he gave the gun to someone, to keep till the heat was off. This someone then travelled to Emerald, 350 kms. up the road, to kill Shirley Edwards, whom they did not know. This did not fit. There was quite a bit missing, there was no connection between Shane Reynolds and Emerald. To top it all off, they could not charge Shane Reynolds, for the other bikie's murder, because he was no longer in the land of the living.

Gerry did not know anybody, from the southern suburbs of the city, he did not even know the southern suburbs, so what was he to do. To save him time he reckoned the best bet was an investigator, so he asked around and found one, he felt he might just trust. His instructions to the investigator, were very clear and precise. Find Danny Bell, in the southern suburbs, and report the findings, complete with photo directly to Gerry. Do not make contact, with the individual. He transferred four hundred dollars into the investigators account to engage his services and said he would be paid handsomely for the information, and no, Gerry was not a hitman, but an accountant. Gerry would expect a result in four working days.

Tom and Eli liked to keep the family together, as much as possible. So now that Gary was a little bigger, and walking, she would bring him down to the lifesavers gatherings, on Saturday mornings, to see what his dad was up to. After lifesaving, they would go up to the council pool. Here Tom would take Gary in his arms, and introduce him to the water. In the beginning it was slow, but it was surprising how quickly, a little fellow like Garry could learn to stay afloat. So this became a ritual, the family would all get into the pool, and slowly Garry learned to move across a short distance, between Tom and Eli. Slowly they increased the distance, between them and Gary made his way across. The way a child learns, at that age, is absolutely mind boggling. From that time they would go to the pool every Saturday, if possible, and Garry learned to be comfortable in the water. Eli had gone back to Taekwondo as soon as she could, to get fit again and loose unnecessary weight, life was always better, when you were feeling good. Just shortly after this particular morning, Eli informed Tom she was expecting again. Tom was overjoyed, what could be better. Eli instinctively, knew when she was pregnant. Before she took the test she had said to herself, she was going to have another baby. She was so happy, having another one of Tom's children, what bliss! This time she did not wait long to tell Bev, but she did ask her to keep it to herself. Since Shirley's passing, and Eli's marriage to Tom, Eli and Bev had become close and spoke to one another multiple times a week.

TWENTY-EIGHT

Rodney was in a bad place, he had a wife and two little girls 11 and seven. He could see no way, of handling this situation. His marriage was not one, where the partners discuss the issues that arise, and work through them, together. Rodney did not, and could not, tell his wife some of the things he had done. He was forced to bottle it up inside. The pressure was mounting, and he did not know, how to cope. It was Friday, so he bought a big bottle of vodka at the off licence, and drove on. Over the weekend, Rodney did not return home. So by the Monday, his wife was frantic, she had no idea where he had got to, and his secretary, was none the wiser. Rodney's absence was reported to the police and Det. Sgt. Adam Poole was quite shocked, he had apparently misread, Rodney, or underestimated his fear. He believed that Rodney would turn up, in a few days, accompanied by a solicitor. Now they were minus, an important witness. They dispatched as many constables, as they could, to look for Rodney. Meanwhile his wife, and some friends of hers, were doing the best they could, to find him. By Friday, there was still no Rodney, and Helen Pleasant, Rodney's wife, was completely distraught, and the girls were just crying, asking what was going on. The local health hub where the doctors and the nurses were stationed, arranged a full time nurse, to Mrs Pleasant and the girls.

It was becoming apparent, that Rodney, must have known much more about Shirley's demise, than the police imagined. The search for Rodney continued without success. What were the police going to do, without the witness? To make it even more difficult, there had been enough rain, to wash away any tyre tracks, that had been made on soil surfaces, alongside tarmac roadways. Right now it looked as if the community of Emerald, needed some divine intervention.

In four days the investigator, still had no answer. So Gerry asked him where he had inquired and his reply was everywhere. Gerry asked if he had tried the council and he replied "yes". Then Gerry said have you been to the Ablution Blocks Cleaning Department in the southern suburbs. The investigator said "no". Gerry said, those employed by this section of the Council were not always very intelligent and were usually engaged by the overseer or foreman. As the turnover could be quite high. These figures were separate from the other information provided by council, with regard to turnover. They were not, readily available figures, for perusal, as it was feared, their disclosure, could very possibly lead, to an unwanted inquiry. An inquiry would serve absolutely no purpose, in easing the situation. So the running of this department, would continue operating as it had up to now. The way things were done in the past, had proven to be the best way. Maintaining a steady successful outcome of the task at hand, without undue interference. Gerry warned the investigator again, not to cause the individual to become aware of this outside interest.

The young married couple moved in with Mrs. Stokes, and they were given the main bedroom and an additional room which they could use as they saw fit. The garage was still in reasonable condition, so Jack parked his vehicle there. He did not use it for work, as he could easily walk the distance. There was only one bathroom, but Mrs. Stokes was unable to use it. A community nurse came each morning to clean her and help dispose of the contents of the portable toilet. These were things, Jack had not known, until now. The room Mrs. Stokes used had been altered to suit her needs, so the young couple were not depriving her of anything. So slowly Jack and Natalie settled in. Jack would rise quietly, kiss his wife goodbye, and be off to the bakery to start a new day. Olaf still came to the shop, but maybe a little later. Jack had grown very fond of the old man, and enjoyed all his stories, plus Olaf made excellent coffee.

It was strange in a way, that Emerald did not have a hospital, but the powers that be, have their own ideas. However it did have a local health hub which did many things the hospitals were disinclined to do. There were three or four doctors depending on the day of the week. There were X ray services, a maternity clinic attached to the hub and four nurses who operated from the hub visiting people in need in the outer areas of the district. As well there was a dentistry section, to deal with dental hygiene. The ambulance station was at the other end of the square.

There were also two junior schools, and a high school, which developed a name, for producing accomplished young men and women who could choose higher education through the University of Arncliffe or pursue a trade by way of the Tafe system. A town like Emerald where the setting, on the coast was idyllic and the weather beautiful, was the stuff that dreams are made of. It was the sort of place that many families, would be more than happy to move to. This was quite noticeable, among blue colour workers, who had slightly different values, to white collar workers, and were keen to have their children experience being near the sea. Many professionals would give an arm and a leg to move there. But it was too late, they were bogged down by their jobs, in the big cities with all the crowds, road traffic jams, and trying to get children to school or sport. It was one continual race to nowhere.

Eli was doing fine, there were no problems, with her pregnancy, and Little Gary was getting bigger by the day. Eli had never imagined, a life like this for herself. She had imagined she would grow old as a spinster. Now look at all, she needed to be grateful for. She thought about the coffee and sandwich bar, she used to have but did not miss it at all. She was just grateful, for what she had learned during those years. She could discuss Tom's work with him, yes it was on a much greater scale, but the basic principles remain the same. Tom felt very blessed nothing was nicer, than coming home to Eli and Gary each afternoon. He was delighted young Gary had reddish hair. Soon there would be four of them, so that will require some thought. There was still one bedroom "empty", although it was not always easy to find. Gary would not need a cot, by the time the new baby arrived, so that was good, but they would need a bed with a pull up side, so he would not fall out in his sleep. They would use a little psychology on Gary, when requiring him to take to the bed. Tom would have to make a serious effort, at cleaning all his paraphernalia out of the room, and moving it into his workshop. In spite of the inconvenience all this was causing, Tom was thoroughly enjoying, the whole affair. He was really blessed having a wife and child now.

Jack and Natalie were doing well and mum (Mrs. Stokes) was enjoying the extra company even if he went to bed at 9 pm. Natalie had envisaged some difficulty in the home situation, but all was good so far. Jack was a considerate person. They both realised this situation had a limited lifespan, in the not too distant future, mum would have to go into proper care. The young couple were careful with their money, and saved some every month. Peter and Leslie had called it quits, as there were just too many incompatibilities, and Peter was not into, arguing and intrigue. Peter appeared happy go lucky, but he was no idiot, he had learned from his father, how to behave and what not to tolerate. He respected everyone, but would not be pushed around, and he did not throw money around. One evening, when he and his dad were closing up for the night, he said to his dad, maybe he would have to run the business, with Michelle when the time came. He said to his dad, that the time he had spent crewing for him, had got rid of any desire on his part, to go fishing again. Peter had little interest in the opposite sex as he had found them to be into drama and intrigue for which he had no time, he was okay on his own. He had plans for his future, but they did not include the female sex. Peter was thinking more, of seeing the interior of the land. In time he would acquire, a good four wheel drive, and slowly kit himself out.

Monday night, Chap arrived for his usual meeting with George. These two had grown to like one another, and they respected each other, for their abilities. Chap asked about the family and Jack and his young bride. George replied all was well. Chap asked George if there was any possibility of buying the building that housed the bakery. George said that the building housed two businesses and quite frankly he had never thought to ask. Chap advised him to make discreet enquiries and tell him about the situation at the next meeting. The balance on the bakery was very small now and George said it would be paid off in the next instalment. Chap was happy to hear this, and said the family had done very well. He departed after finishing his double black label Johnny Walker.

With regard to the security Tom felt, they needed to make another move. One of the three big factory jobs had just been secured, and there was a good chance they would win a second one. He asked Craig what he thought they needed most. Craig said another electrician just to help with the call outs on the domestic front. Tom said okay, source another electrician and you will have to become more involved in the securing of these big factory complexes with me. In a domestic security setup, the sensors are positioned at waist height, usually around the perimeter of the rooms. As each sensor receives and sends the signal this pattern is carried out throughout the house making the house a sealed unit. The control box is usually positioned near the main entrance for convenience. Here the system can be activated or turned off as required. Once activated if someone should cut the beam an alarm is activated. Telling the homeowner all is not well. He needs to investigate and call the number of the security firm, which would be relayed to the electrician on standby, to investigate. Should a member of the household move some furniture blocking the beam, then the system will not become active and the security company will need to be called. This is part of the maintenance, for which the homeowners pay a quarterly or yearly fee. This also gives the owner, options on up dated improvements, as they become available, at a special price.

In the case of a factory premises, everything is on a much larger scale. The sensors have to emit a much stronger beam because of distances involved, and the control unit is much larger, so the setup is much more powerful and complicated. The factory staff have to have access during the day, but after work, the system has to be set. If there is one box, or crate, or anything else, blocking a beam the system will not become active. So Tom needs to take into account, along with the management, the areas which are most often used, and those which are more permanent. It is imperative, that management realised, Tom is not a magician, and tries to work with him. Many places painted lines on the floor, to show the workers, where the goods need to be stacked.

This makes the factory system much more complex and more expensive. These have a phone line from the factory that connects to the police department as well as to Tom. As would be expected, a break in at a factory is usually done, by more than one individual. This requires the police to respond in numbers, to limit the possibility of being overpowered, by a group of thugs. However if you value your products, then this is undoubtedly the best way to go. To date, there had only been one attempted, break in, on one of Tom's systems, and it was a drunk oblivious to what he was doing. In a way this was good, as it was reported in the local newspaper, which helped people understand this was a no no.

TWENTY-NINE

Three weeks after Rodney's disappearance, the police in Emerald received a call, from a fellow who went down to Lattis Bay to fish, and found a motor car with a deceased man in it. Two police were immediately dispatched to the site. Sure enough the occupant was deceased, and there was a pipe leading from the exhaust, into the cabin of the car. The coroner was informed, as well as the ambulance services. The policemen checked the car registration, with base, and sure enough it was Rodney's car. At this stage it was not possible to identify Rodney, because of decomposition. Det. Sgt. Adam Poole made his way down there, to inspect the scene, and was upset by this waste of life. Rodney must have felt stuck between a rock and a hard place, to have taken this way out. This was not good for their investigation, as they felt Rodney was an eye witness, to the slaying of Shirley

Edwards. After the forensic team had completed their examination of the site. The coroner had the body placed in the ambulance, and sent back to the mortuary. So far, there was no confirmed proof it was Rodney. Most of those on site, believed in their hearts, it must be Rodney, but it was the duty of the coroner to announce this. Adam Poole went to the house, where Helen Pleasant and her two girls were staying, and informed Helen, a body had been found, and he believed it to be Rodney. However he was waiting for the coroner, to confirm the findings. Adam was reluctant to say anything further at this stage, but said he would get back to her, as soon as he knew more.

It was not long, before Gerry found out about Rodney's demise, from Sgt. Lewis. This complicated things. Now there was only one possible witness, and they needed him desperately, to solve this terrible murder, of Shirley. Gerry notified his friend Tom, of the finding, and said to say nothing to the girls. Later that day, the coroner made an announcement, to the effect that Rodney's body had been found down at Lattis Bay. Helen was completely overcome by this news, when Adam informed her, and Adam was very saddened, to watch this poor lady, smitten with this terrible wave, of grief. This outcome had not been necessary, if Rodney had just spoken to his wife, this could probably have been avoided. The coroner released the body, to the family to make arrangements for his funeral. Apparently, Rodney had driven all the way to Lattis Bay, and then connected a hose from the exhaust into the car, with the engine running, and sat there drinking vodka from a bottle. Slowly he was overcome by fumes and died, the engine must have kept going until it ran out of fuel. There was no proof, of Rodney being involved in any way, with Shirley's death, maybe some would be forthcoming in time. To Gerry, this was a big blow, he had hoped to get Rodney, to see sense and tell all. Now, there was just one very precious witness, who was somewhere in the southern suburbs of the big city. If they could not get hold of Danny Bell, and bring him back to Emerald, to give testimony against Spider Kelly, then Spider would not be charged for the murder of Shirley Edwards, and that must just never happen.

Four days after the coroner released the body. Rodney was laid to rest in the local cemetery, with very few people to see him off. It was a very sad day, in Emerald's history, as it was the second person to lose their life, in the saga of Shirley's demise. Helen and the children were now living with Helen's mum, and Helen was finding the going very tough. The town had helped, by taking up a collection, to help pay for the funeral. Three days later, Spider heard about Rodney's suicide and felt absolutely nothing for him, Spider was a cold fish. One had to be, to do the things he did. Now there was just Danny Bell, and nobody knew where he was, so that was okay.

Gerry was very lucky, as he was sitting wondering how best to proceed when, he received a call from the investigator saying, he had found Danny and he had a photo to prove it. Gerry arranged to meet him at a coffee shop, on the road down towards Eight Mile Beach. Gerry parked his car among others there, so the investigator would not know which one was his, and waited at a table until the investigator arrived. Gerry transferred the photo from the investigator's phone to his, and was given the information about where he worked, and his residential address. He then deleted the information from the investigator's mobile and returned it to the investigator. Gerry paid the investigator a further five hundred dollars by mobile transfer and he waited till the investigator left, before returning home. Gerry was very pleased with this information, and had to decide how to use it.

This really needed to be handled very carefully,

he could not afford to screw this up, or things could turn rather nasty between him, and Sgt. Lewis. Gerry felt, he needed to talk to Bev in confidence, to make sure he had her backing. That evening while Jane was doing her homework in her room Gerry discussed the situation with Bev. He told her, he had found Danny Bell. At first Bev could not believe him. He told her, he had engaged a private detective, to go down to the big city and find him. It had taken him some time, but he had been successful. He said he would have to go down, and get him and bring him back to Emerald, to testify against Spider. He made Bev promise to say nothing, to anybody. He would be going down to get him, as soon as he could organise an open day, with his secretary. He got his secretary in next morning, and asked her how booked up his calendar was, she said there were a few appointments, but these could be rescheduled, if he wished. Gerry told her, he would not be in the next day, at all.

Next morning, armed with a street directory of the big city, and the GPS in the car. Gerry kissed his wife and said "wish me luck" promising to phone her, he set off for the big city. He felt he would go as far as he could, and then reassess the situation. Gerry was surprised how well he did, as in certain areas of the city the streets took twists and turns, as if they knew where he wanted to go. By ten thirty he had found the offices of the cleaning department, of the southern suburbs, he was looking for. He felt extremely pleased because for the last couple of blocks, he had just followed the road, not knowing where he was going. Fortunately, he ended up at the right place. These council buildings were very old, and of a design uncommon these days. These, facilities would date back many years, as in modern times there were no such conveniences. It was admirable, that they were still kept in good condition. Now to find Danny Bell. He thought about it for a while and then decided, he would just go in and ask for him.

The manager seemed a decent type and Gerry spoke to him for a while saying how difficult it was coming from up north to find these offices. Then Gerry introduced himself and asked if Danny Bell still worked there and Joe Styles (the manager) said "yes he did, Would Gerry like to speak to him" (wow! what a question) "yes please" said Gerry. Joe got up from his seat and strolled to the door and pointed at a building two doors down and said you will find him in there cleaning. Gerry thanked Joe and made his way to the ablution building, Joe had pointed out. He hesitated for a moment, and said to himself, here goes, and walked into the building. About halfway down he could see someone busy cleaning. He approached the person, and as he raised his head Gerry recognised Danny. Gerry said "how is it going"? Danny replied "Not bad, I'm nearly finished now." "Well," said Gerry, "I seem to be a little lost, would you like to show me, where we can get something to eat and drink."

Danny put away his cleaning materials, and washed up, and came back to Gerry. "I am Danny Bell" he said and Gerry introduced himself. They walked up a couple of blocks and turned left into a main street, "Up here there is a real good place," Danny said. They walked into the restaurant, and Gerry could see it looked acceptable, it was clean, with few people inside. They sat down at a table in the far corner, and looked at the menu, "pick whatever you fancy Danny," Gerry said. Danny wanted a burger, fries and a coke. Gerry said he would have a cappuccino and a ham and tomato sandwich. So while they were waiting for their order, Gerry asked how it was going here. Danny replied "much more peaceful here, could not take that madness of Spider any more."Gerry said "I agree Spider is bad news, but did Danny know,

Spider was now inside for four years, for some of his crimes." "Well that's real good " Danny said.

The food arrived and Danny wasted no time attacking the burger. They were quiet for a while and then Danny blurted out, "but they need to get him for that lovely lady he shot". Gerry nearly choked, he did not, expect that. He replied "did he really do that"? Danny said "yes I saw him do it, it upset me very much that is why I came back here. I knew I could not go to the police because he would kill me too. So I came back here as soon as I could, but it is not right what he did". Gerry said the police were busy getting all the information together to put him in jail for a long long time. Danny said he was happy to hear that. Gerry asked him if he would like to help, do this for the sake of that lovely lady he killed. Danny said, "he would like to help, as what Spider did was very, very bad and his mother thought so too". "I have an idea" Gerry said "we will tell your boss you have been called away on official business. Then you can pick up some things at your digs, and we will return to Emerald." It worked like a charm, Danny was a simple young fellow with a lower than average I.Q. but his mum had taught him right from wrong. When Spider went off the rails Danny did not know what to do, so he went home, as soon as he could break away from Spider.

They loaded Danny's small case, in the boot of Gerry's car, and retraced Gerry's steps to Emerald. They spoke about many things, on the way back to Emerald. Gerry had time to phone his wife and say all good, we will be home soon. When they neared Emerald, Gerry phoned Sgt. Fred Lewis and asked him to meet him, at the steps of the police station in 15 minutes. Gerry told Danny "we are going to see Sgt. Fred Lewis, and he is a real cool guy, and he will help you put all the things you know and saw, on paper to give to the judge". At the police station, Gerry got out the car first and told Danny, just to wait a minute. Fred was waiting for them. "You have to be gentle with this guy. He is like an eight year old, in some respects, do not get rough with him. He will tell you everything you need to know". Gerry said "if you wish to speak to him now, I would like to be present as he trusts me." Fred thought about that for a minute and agreed, as it would only be a preliminary interview.

THIRTY

Gerry got home late that day, exhausted, but very pleased with the results. It sure looked as if Spider was for the high jump. He knew Fred, but he was not, so sure about Adam Poole. He was concerned, Adam might get rough with Danny who was a simple fellow and that would be counterproductive. Given the opportunity, Danny would tell all he knew. As he would never be an adult mentally, Gerry told Fred it would be a blot on society, if he was in any way held as an accessory, to the murder of Shirley. He had no idea what Spider was up to. Gerry apologised to Adam the following day, for going straight to Fred, but he said both he and Fred knew Danny Bell, from past experience, and they were worried he might clam up dealing with a policeman, he did not know. Gerry told Adam that Danny was completely childlike in some things, and he would not tell lies. He had obtained a drivers licence but that was after being extensively schooled over a period of time and he had never had an accident.

Danny was put into protective custody, and his name was not used again. As his evidence was immensely important. He was housed in a flat, owned by the Department of Homeland Securities, to be used in cases like this. A single female Constable Moira Higgins, would be his companion at present, until a suitable male constable, became available. X was loaded into the car, while it was in the garage, at the flat and told to lie on the back seat. On arrival at the police station the vehicle was driven into the enclosed yard, where X could emerge from the car safely. Every effort had to be made, that Spider did not find out, about X being a witness. Furthermore nobody would be told, he was in Emerald, except those that already knew. Danny would be known as witness X.

Later, Fred asked Gerry how he knew where X was, and he said he did not know, he just started looking, until he found him. Gerry told Tom, swearing him to secrecy, and he was very happy to hear that, but he would not tell Eli until the trial. Gerry assured Tom the witness statement they were getting, from X would be very comprehensive, as he seemed to have a photographic memory, when it came to certain things. Possibly it was the more evil events, he remembered best. Tom was very impressed with his friends tenacity.

The interviews took place every morning, and afternoon for about an hour and a half. When X became tired he just said so, and they would get him a coke or burger. He was allowed to watch movies for a while, until he was ready to talk again. The idea of doing it slowly at X's pace, paid dividends. The volume of information, was staggering. While treated well, X was a very pleasant person with good manners. These were obviously taught to him, by his mother, as he often referred to her when mentioning, one or other behaviour. X's recall was quite outstanding. He remembered the day Jack punched Spider, at the bakery and put him lights out, on the pavement. Spider asked who had hit him, and X replied he could not see, who the person was who hit him. He spoke about the time in Eden and the trouble Spider made there, beating guys up. He said after the shooting of the lovely lady down near the fisherman's co-op, he decided he had to get away from Spider. However he did not get a chance because Spider kept him close by, all the time. He believed Spider could see X wanted, out. However one day in Emerald, shortly after they returned from Eden. Spider had run out of weed, so he needed to go out, to get some. It was early in the morning and he believed X was still asleep, but he was wrong. As soon as Spider left the house, Danny bundled his meagre possessions into his Subaru and left, as quickly as possible. X was on his way home where he believed Spider would never find him. He was right, and Spider would not bother looking, he would find someone else, to ferry him around.

"In the beginning Spider was not too bad, but the drugs just made him worse. X said, he did not do drugs, as his mum told him they were very bad. It was good driving Spider around in the beginning until he realised, Spider was not interested in him just the transport. Now all he wanted was to do his job as a cleaner, and be safe." The total interviews took a week, as they had to have many breaks to keep X happy. The results were phenomenal. It was hard to believe that X could remember such detail.

Adam and Fred spoke to the public prosecutor, about how they were going to proceed with the case, as they were concerned for X's safety. They had all the statements on tape and video, but for his safety, they did not want X to appear in court. The public prosecutor, aware of the fact that Spider would do anything, to have this charge dropped, approached judge Mason, who had presided over the previous Spider Kelly case, about the safety of X. Judge Mason said, this case was far more important than the previous case, so they would definitely have to protect X. The prosecutor pointed out there were still associates of Spider, in town, and the police did not want X to be attacked by them. Judge Mason asked where he was being held now and they told him, in the special facilities provided by the department.

The judge said it was necessary for X to watch the trial on video, so that he could see and appreciate, the testimony he had given, was taking Spider down. However, he would not be viewed by the court at the trial. So the authorities would need to make provision for that. Judge Mason said preparations, should go ahead and the prosecutor should have all his paperwork ready, for trial in three weeks time, Monday 18th July. There was no need for delay, as X was the main witness. The prosecutor reported back to Adam, that it was a go. This was received very favourably, by Fred Lewis and his constables. Then Fred put through a call to Gerry to tell him the good news, Gerry was over the moon about this development, and told Tom who was very grateful, to Gerry for his hard work. As constable Higgins was required for other duties, they replaced her with Constable Mattock a big strong young fellow. Provision was made for X to watch the trial on a screen in one of the offices with Constable Mattock present. Sergeants Poole and Lowe were concerned that Spider's accomplices, in the area might have become suspicious, with the extra movement on the go, that the police had found X. This could be dangerous and they did not want to alarm X

The first thing Spider knew about the upcoming trial, was when the prison warder told him his lawyer, was there to see him. Brendan Lock introduced himself, and told Spider he had been instructed, to represent Spider in the case, where he was being charged with the murder of Shirley Edwards. Fortunately Spider had just had some marijuana and was feeling good. He managed, after swallowing a couple of times, to try, and get control of the situation. "and when, is this supposed to be taking place."Spider asked, "In three weeks time" replied Brendan. "Well then I shall require, some time to formulate my defence" said Spider. " I need time to think about this, as I cannot remember everything off the top of my head. Give me five days to see what I can remember, and come back and see me".

Spider had a number of contacts that he would need, to help him find his way out of this predicament. Trying to get out through the sick bay, was quite difficult as it had been tried before, unsuccessfully. Spider had a contact in the library, who received some weed from him, so he would have to be quizzed, maybe he had some ideas. His contact in the laundry department might just be able to help, with this problem. He sent a message to Larry for an urgent meeting, this would be held in the ablution block. Someone could be positioned, to alert them of anybody approaching. Spider was surprised how in control he felt, at the moment but that could change if he was unable to extricate himself from this sorry situation.

Somebody had found Danny, there was no other explanation for the present drama. Danny must have told them everything, and now they were after his blood. He had no defence, what could he claim as extenuating circumstances. The only way out of this horrible mess, was to escape and move far from the district. There was no way he was going to serve an additional 30 years in jail. Spider was waiting for Larry, as he arrived. Spider wasted no time in telling Larry, he needed to get out by coming Thursday. As the cops wanted to nail him, for a further 30 years.

"What day does the laundry go for cleaning" Spider asked Larry and Larry said "usually Wednesday morning, about 10 am." "Well how difficult would it be for me to go out mixed in the dirty laundry" asked Spider. "Not impossible" said Larry but it requires a group of six, to achieve the feat, as all the warders present, have to be distracted. Spider gave Larry six zolls of weed and asked him to check out, if they could do it. If it was possible there, would be much more weed.

Once Larry had gone he got hold of warder, Rudy and asked him to get him a handcuff key. All of this was costing Spider, but he had the connection on the outside, feeding him the drugs to get these favours done. In prison everything had a price, you just needed to be able to afford it. In this case it was vitally important to Spider, that he escape as a further 30 years in prison, would see the end of him. Spider's crew outside owed him, so they would go along with his crazy scheme. In the past he had delivered, even now while in jail, he was running his business on the outside.

The police in Emerald were on full alert during this pretrial period, as it was possibly the time when Spider would try to escape, so as not to stand trial. The prison was 10 kilometres out of Emerald.

If Spider was going to try something, it would probably be between the prison and the court. So everybody involved in the case was briefed as to the importance of the next few weeks.

The scene was set for the following Wednesday, Spider had negotiated a deal with warder Rudy, and inmate Larry, who held a position of some importance in the prison. Spider gave warder Rudy a message, in code, to give to his man on the outside. Eddie, was to get, three arms of weed and deliver them, to Cecil the driver of the laundry truck down at the laundry depot, by Tuesday 5 p.m. An arm of weed was a parcel of marijuana about the same size as a man's forearm.

The laundromat was owned by Cecil and Clive Went, and the two had been residents of Emerald for many years. Neither of them married, and they seemed content with each other's company. They had owned the brewery, in the old days, however when they could no longer meet the requirements for a brewery, they changed the setup into a laundry. They subsequently got the contracts for the hotels and the prison to attend to their laundry requirements. Now the laundry truck had been many things, in it's time. It had transported liquor, when the present laundry depot had been a brewery. It was an old

Bedford which had, one sets of small wheels either side at the back. This had made it easier, to load the cartons of liquor, onto the lower back deck by hand. Then it was used for transporting bales of hay, for the dairy cows, during the terrible drought. Since that time, it had been used to transport pallets of bricks, and this had destroyed the deck surface. So the deck was replaced, and then it was decided to raise the deck, as it served no further purpose being so low. In doing so, uprights were run the length of the deck at suitable intervals and noggins spaced in between the uprights as strengtheners. The top was made up of planks running across the width of the deck, at front and back and in the centre they had planks running from front to back. During the construction, provision was made for a place of concealment, in the middle of the deck. At the back of the truck, noggins were inserted between the uprights, preventing any inspection, of the interior of the back deck. Because the Bedford had been so low at the back originally, it's present appearance did not seem strange. Looking from the back, it was not possible to see the deck had been raised. The ends between the two levels were blocked off with pieces of timber. In the middle of the deck, was a loose plank, that could be raised, if you knew how.

This cavity was used to smuggle various illegal items, including liquor, weed and anything else that was required by inmates, when necessary. The cavity was big enough, to accommodate a man provided he, was not too thickset.

THIRTY-ONE

The plan of action was, two of the three arms of weed, would be concealed in this cavity at the laundry, on the Wednesday concerned. The third arm was payment, to Cecil and Cyril for the use of the truck, to smuggle Spider out of prison. At the prison when off loading the laundry baskets, the weed would be delivered, to warder Rudy. He in conjunction with Larry, would see each participant, in the operation received his cut, after Spider was concealed in the cavity, as the truck was loaded with the dirty laundry. At the prison, two inmates got into a brawl near the loading bay, for the laundry baskets, with the result that, all attention was focused on the brawl. A further three managed to drop a basket, while loading, and one inmate hurt his shoulder. The baskets were first loaded, on the side the warders could see, from where they stood. Once this was accomplished, Spider was slipped quietly, into the cavity under the middle plank, which the warders could not see.

Once all the baskets were in place and secured, a warder climbed up on the back of the truck, and pushed a rod into each basket, to ensure nobody was trying to escape. The all clear was issued, and the truck was allowed to leave. Although the journey was very bumpy, Spider was not complaining, he would be free in a very short time. On the arrival of the truck at the laundromat, the courtyard gates were closed. Cecil supervised the off loading of the baskets, from the truck onto the concrete slab at the entrance, to the laundry which was the same height, as the back of the Bedford truck. The baskets had big castors underneath them to facilitate moving them, particularly around the laundry. Cecil and Cyril had introduced some automation to help move the heavy baskets, as they were getting on in age. Neither of them, could move a basket fully laden. Once all was clear Cecil walked onto the back of the truck and lifted the plank granting Spider, freedom. Spider thanked Cecil, something he very seldom did. Cecil had an arm of the weed for the job, so he was smiling. Cecil told Spider, he should leave the laundry premises as soon as possible, as they did not want to be implicated.

Eddie would come around to pick Spider up as soon the coast was clear. As there were no classes on a Wednesday, Spider would not be missed until roll call at 6 p.m. However, Spider was keen to move to his old digs, at the "Dairy Land", as he still had a considerable amount of money and other things secreted there. Eddie was clever enough, to arrive, in a car he did not normally drive, go into the laundry business and come out, with what looked like pressed laundry. While this was going on, Spider carefully managed to get into the back of the car, and cover himself with a rug lying there. Spider instructed Eddie to take him up towards the "Dairy Land", and he was dropped off, where there was still plenty of bush. He told Eddie to come back once it was dark, driving down towards the dunes at the end of the property and he would be there. Bring hamburgers, water and weed, he would be paid then.

Spider made his way carefully to the "Dairy Land", and could immediately see someone was showing interest in the property. The fencing had been improved and once inside it was apparent some timber had been removed. He hastened to his different hiding places to see if his things were still there. His money, which was a substantial amount, was untouched but someone had taken one of his knives. It was obvious he could not stay here, the police would come here first. After dark Spider waited out the back near the bushes, and Eddie arrived, bringing all Spider required at the moment. Spider wasted no time digging into the hamburgers, fortunately Eddie had the sense to bring some beer as well. Spider paid Eddie, and said he should return the next morning, and drive up to the sports fields further, up towards the cemetery and he would be near the club house. He should bring some sandwiches, and coffee as well as more weed. He would then explain his plan.

Eddie said Tollie, one of the runners had seen a BMW bring someone back to the police station about two weeks prior. Spider said he was aware of that, and was very keen to knife that guy. Eddie asked if he knew, who the guy was and Spider said "OH YES, I do". He told Eddie he needed a rucksack filled with food, and some water and a plenty of weed. He asked Eddie if he knew of a place he could hide, for a couple of days. Eddie said "yes there is an old shack up at the cemetery. It is at the far end towards the beach, and is not obvious from the road". Spider said "Eddie should return that night, and he would find Spider there, bring more hamburgers and he would make his own way there." Spider worked his way over to the cemetery, without being detected, and forced his way into the shack. It was furnished with an old bed and a stool, neither of them looked very strong. He sat on the stool and it held. Then he tried the old bed it also withstood his weight. The only conclusion he could come to was, Eddie had used this place on occasion.

Thinking about what the accountant had done. Bringing Danny back to give evidence against Spider. Infuriated him to such an extent that he decided he would have to deal with Gerry before moving on. Spider was very determined, to kill the accountant, for finding Danny, after he left the area. He had made it possible for the police, to extract all the information from Danny, about the slaying of that woman. He had the gall to try, and put one over Spider. Everything was going well, until he decided to stick his nose into the affair. He needed to pay for the trouble he had caused Spider. Nobody should think they can step into his life, and derail it. He would pay the ultimate price, and then Spider would disappear forever. He would go north and find another town, where he could start his business up again causing pain, and misery to all who dealt with him. Spider's approach, was very straight forward he was the ONLY, individual of any significance, everybody else was dispensable. It seems Spider had become the ultimate narcissist, unable to recognise the fact that everybody had a right to live, and satisfy their needs and desires. Spider had passed the point of no return, no amount of talking would convince him that he was just a single individual, in a world full of people. The only safe place for Spider was prison.

Roll call, in the prison had come and gone, - and there was no Spider. The chief warder was furious how could this have happened. He assembled his warders in front of him and proceeded to threaten them with prosecution, if they did not come up, with an answer. In spite of this stern talking to there seemed to be no answer. All the staff said they had no idea what had happened. The chief warder got his security staff to go through the videos for the day from morning roll call, to see if they could find any abnormality. However there was very little to report. There had been a confrontation in the ablution block, between three inmates over some cigarettes, in the morning. A fight had broken out between two inmates before the laundry truck was leaving, and at dinner time one of the enforcers tipped over another inmates tray of food. The cameras were programmed to go to any sudden action, and this is what the cameras did. These were all normal everyday events, when you had over one hundred men confined to a small space, and they did not wish to be there. You can not shoot them all, because you are angry. It was not even certain, if Spider had inside help to escape. The assistance could possibly have come from outside, as no one knew when he had disappeared.

Eli's time to have her baby came due, and she gave birth to a beautiful little girl, weighing 3.5kilos, without suffering any complications. Both mother and baby were pronounced fit and well, and the baby wasted no time, letting everybody know she was there. Now it was Eli's turn, to name the baby. Little Gary who was just over two years old now, was actually hoping the baby might be a bit bigger so they could wrestle on the lounge carpet, but it seemed that would have to wait a while. Tom was very happy with the addition to the family and beamed. Bev, Gerry, and Neve along with Don were excited and wanted to meet the little girl. Tom promised to pick up Don the next day to pay a visit. They were allowed to see her the following day, for a short while, and were thrilled at the lovely addition to Tom's family. As it was Eli's chance to name her baby girl, and Tom was waiting patiently to hear what his daughter would be called.

Tom was in the process of reassessing his situation with regards to work and family. He was now blessed with a beautiful wife and two lovely children, how does it help if he spends most of his time at work, to the detriment of his loved ones. He had two very sound businesses which were doing very well, he was not in debt. Maybe it was time to invest some finance, into other ventures to produce income, which did not require an input of time. He had a small block of six two bedroom flats, that would be fully paid up in one month. The "dairy land" up at the north end of Emerald was a work in process, from the point of view that he and Gerry, owned it outright, and were not under any pressure to develop it now. Once Eli was back home again, they could have a good talk about their future.

The chief warder was on to the police immediately, he was certain Spider had escaped. The constable put the call through to Sgt. Fred Lewis who nearly hit the ceiling when he heard the news.

He asked when this happened, and how it occurred but the chief warder was unable to answer these questions very accurately. So Sgt. Lewis said "you mean you do not know"? The Chief Warder replied that it had occurred since roll call at 6 am. This was not much help for the police, as they would now have to have a full scale search. All police stations up and down the coast, were notified of a dangerous prisoner on the loose, with a detailed description and photo forwarded to each station. In Emerald, all police were called back on duty, to take part in the search for Spider. As a result of this escape the Detective Inspector Barry Wallis along with Sergeant Adam Poole were on their way up from the big city, to coordinate the search. There was much said about the prison employees, which was not fit for publication, and their reputation sank to an all time low. In spite of everything the Chief Warder said, there was no help forthcoming from the warders probably because they did not know, or had been paid to say nothing. None of them wished to meet Spider up a dark alley anytime soon.

Eli was back home, and very grateful to be there. Tom had taken time off to bring her home from the maternity ward, along with the new edition to the family. Gary was very happy to have his sister home, but she was still not big enough to play with him. Eli was very lucky her second baby was just as contented as Gary had been, surely this must come from the mother's disposition, what else. It was not long before the subject of the little girl's name came up, and Tom ventured to ask Eli if she had given it any thought. Eli said she had thought about, and felt that she would like to call her Shirley May Edwards. Well! Tom could not speak for a moment while he registered what Eli had just said, and then he embraced her and said he would like that very much. So the christening was arranged for the following month, to give Eli some time to recuperate. One Saturday when Don and the Keane family were all present, as well as some of Eli's friends from the Coffee and Sandwich Bar that Eli had run. Shirley May Edwards was christened. Don was quite emotional when he heard the baby would be named after his daughter, Shirley, and he told Tom he appreciated that very much. They all went around to Tom and Eli's home afterwards for some refreshments and photos. Tom made a point of taking a photo of Don holding little Shirley, with his mobile. He had that blown up to a 150mm x 100 mm and framed it, and gave it to Don. Gary asked his dad when he would be able to play with Shirley and Tom was obliged to tell him, "not for a little while yet, but you can play with me."

The police force was in a state of turmoil, how were they going to apprehend Spider, there were no leads. The Went brothers, Clive and Cecil had been cross examined by the police over some time, and it was felt that they knew nothing. It did not really make sense for them to get involved, they had a lot to lose and little to gain. They were making a comfortable living out of the laundry business, why stick your neck out? As for the warders, well, how would they accomplish something like this? If they did, they would be found out and they would pay a heavy price. Keeping things going along nicely was far safer, and it did not affect the blood pressure. The police believed Spider would have fled the district, as he was well known around Emerald.

One Saturday afternoon as Eli and Tom were sitting outside with young Gary, enjoying his antics, while Shirley was asleep having just been fed. Tom said to Eli, he had been looking at all they had, including two beautiful children, and he realised that he was missing out on their growing up, being at work for most of the day. He felt he needed to be present now, to see and enjoy his children growing up. When they were 17 and off to university, it was too late. He wanted to know his children, and he wanted them to know him. Eli could not agree more, what a child learns in it's first seven years is vitally important.

What exactly is the idea of having children, if you see them at bed time in the week? If Tom worked from 9am to 2pm and then comes home surely he will have the best of both worlds. Eli had been talking about daycare for Gary. Well Tom felt alarmed at this, he had hardly had time to enjoy this bundle of tricks, and there was talk of sending him to daycare. Tom felt strongly that before they started school he wanted to know them better. He mentioned to Eli that he would like Shirley to start in the pool with them as soon as practical. Tom wanted his children to be good swimmers, and comfortable in the water. Once they were at junior school he could tailor his working day accordingly. Eli liked what she heard, any help with the children would be well received. Children learn from their parents, they see what goes on and soak it all up, so being there for them in their formative years, is surely of paramount importance.

A good example of what can go wrong is visible for all to see. Homeless children running around when they should be at school or with their mother. Yes, it is easy to talk about these things but, maybe if parents were able to devote more time to the upbringing of their children, things might be better all around. Tom realised he was in an enviable position as he could do more for his children's upbringing than many. So he should accept the responsibility, and help his two to have the best opportunity possible for success in life. So it was agreed by Tom and Eli that Tom would begin tailoring his office hours to see more of Gary and little Shirley. First, however he needed to make some changes at work.

****

Over in Tegwans' Nest life went on and the local business was doing well again after the earlier invasion of their domain, by the police. The fact that some of the fellows had had the foresight to remove a large quantity of plants from the area, saved a lot of further hassle. The warning system was working. The new crop was looking good and at present the police were very busy trying to find Spider, who had escaped from jail. Harvesting would soon begin, so the product should bring a sizeable amount, of much needed cash. This is not to say that police had not looked at rubbish disposal trucks as means of transport for the weed, however they could find no reason to suspect them.

There had been no sightings of Spider anywhere, and the police were very frustrated. For fear of their lives, the runners were saying nothing, and it was doubtful they were aware of his location. Spider was keeping well out of the way of the police, but he was aware of their presence. His insane passion was to take revenge on the BMW driver (Gerry Keane), for having the cheek to interfere in the events that were, absolutely none of his concern. Engineering the return of Danny Bell who knew all there was to know about Spider, and his terrible deeds. If it had not been for this interference, Spider believed he would have done his four years and been totally free. According to Eddie, one of the runners, he believed that the owner of the BMW and his friend would meet at the private bar of George's Hotel once a week for a beer, but he did not know which day it was. Spider believed if he could attack Gerry outside the pub as he was leaving he could settle the score.

Tom went down to Edwards Security to see how Craig was getting on with the new electrician. Craig said he was doing fine. He was being instructed by one of the other electricians and he seemed to be absorbing the facts very well. The other electricians would take him out on some call to see how to behave and then he would be on his own. Craig said he had good reports on him from others that had worked with him so he was confident the new man would blend in. Tom told Craig to mobile him if necessary.

At the solar shop there was plenty of hustle and bustle. Brian had primed the new installers, and they were on their way out to do their first installation. Gerard, the new electrician was going with them to make sure they measured out, the position the panels correctly. So far so good. Tom discussed how many jobs were pending and Brian said 10. This was about what they were working with, as it fluctuated between ten and four. This was okay, time would tell how to adjust the programme.. While they were talking Brian brought up the fact that they would require a ute to bring back the first team of installers from a job as the second team would have the truck with them. There were situations where the two jobs were quite far apart, and they would not be completed at the same time. Tom agreed with this and said he would see to it right away. Tom went to the office and did some checking on the internet and came back and told Brian, when he was free, Tom and he would go down town hire a ute, and get some additional ladders. Tom told Brian to keep him informed how the installation went, and left

It was now five days that Spider had been waiting, for his opportunity to get at Gerry. Maybe tonight, he might be lucky. It was already dark and Spider was being driven, by Eddie. He told him to drive up Avery Lane and stop, just before the intersection with Wallis street. It is very difficult to imagine a person so obsessed with revenge, that he was incapable of any form of practical reasoning. To the extent that he was throwing away any chance of escape, in favour of a futile attempt, to kill the man he had built up, an insane vengeance against. Any sane person would have fled the area, in an effort to remain free, but not Spider. He was going to be, his own downfall come what may. Eddie did as instructed and killed the engine on stopping. Spider slowly got out of the car, he had and eight inch dagger with him. This did not look good, Spider approached the corner, concealing himself behind some bushes. He could see two men standing talking near the entrance to the courtyard, that led to the private bar. One was Gerry and he was furthest from Spider, Tom was standing facing towards the entrance of the courtyard. They were reasonably close together, but Spider was only interested in Gerry. At this stage Spider, could still have decided the odds were stacked against him, and he could have withdrawn and fled the district.

THIRTY-TWO

He believed he could cross the few metres that separated him from Gerry in a flash and destroy him. This could only be described as, an act of inpenetrable stupidity. Spider launched himself in Gerry's direction, and Tom reacted instinctively, pushing Gerry back so that he fell. While this was happening George had been standing under the archway at the beginning of the courtyard. George knew how to move quickly, and this he did getting onto Spider's back, and forcing him to the ground. However the momentum of Spider's lunge carried him close enough to Gerry to inflict some serious damage. With George on his back, Spider was going nowhere now. Gerry had not been so lucky, he had sustained, a gash to his upper left arm, the gash was deep, and quite long. Spider had managed to reach Gerry with his out stretched arm and inflict a serious wound. George shouted to Peter to bring some bandages from the first aid pronto. It was bad, the gash was deep and they battled to stop the blood flow. Both the police and the ambulance were there in record time. The medics took over helping Gerry, taking him straight to Eden Hospital. When the police arrived George was still sitting on Spider's back preventing him from, committing further destruction. The dagger lay on the dirt just out of Spider's reach. Meanwhile Eddie had fled the scene in his car. The drug trade had just suffered a major body blow, hopefully terminal.

Spider was handcuffed, shackled, and put in the back of the police wagon, and taken to the police station. The dagger was placed in a bag and taken as evidence to the dreadful deed. On arrival, Spider was booked in, then he was stripped, and his body was searched for any concealed handcuff keys or blades. He then had the pleasure, of donning prison garb again, and being placed in an inner cell, one without external walls. Sgt. Lewis made it very clear this guy, was not going to escape again. He was to be checked every half hour. Meanwhile Sgt. Poole and Inspector Barry Wallis were very relieved, they could return to base.

There was much more concern for Gerry. Having called Bev and told her about Gerry's condition,

Tom rushed to Eden Hospital to find out how Gerry was doing. They had managed to stop the bleeding the doctors, were assessing whether he should be transported to the big city, because of the damage to the ligaments and tendons. After an assessment by the doctors, Gerry was flown down to the big city by chopper, for the surgeons to reattach the tendons and ligaments. This operation was performed, immediately on his arrival, as any delay would make the situation far more complicated. By early morning Gerry was out of theatre, but very groggy and he was on strong medication for the pain. He had received 30 stitches in his left upper arm, and it was bandaged to protect against infection. The doctors said that it was thanks to, the immediate actions of Tom and George, as well as the medics that he survived. He could have bled out at the scene, had it not been for their quick actions.

The very quick reactions of Tom and George had prevented a death at the scene. Tom pushing Gerry backwards and George flattened Spider, had in actual fact saved Gerry from certain death. When Tom pushed Gerry backwards Spider knew he could not stab Gerry in the heart, he lowered his arm and made an upward motion catching Gerry in the left upper arm. Gerry remained in hospital, and he now had over two litres of somebody else's blood, flowing through his veins. Bev and Jane had gone through a terrible time, as they arrived in Eden, Gerry was being flown out to the big city, for emergency treatment. They returned home and Tom told them, Gerry would likely be down south for four or five days at least. Bev called Gerry's sister to tell her about the event and ask, if she could stay there for a couple of nights. This was agreed and Bev would fly from Arncliffe in the morning, while Jane would stay with a friend from school. Tom had told Eli of the incident before he drove to Eden, he now went home with a heavy heart.

By lunchtime next day the news was Gerry, was out of intensive care and was doing fine. At present he could not use his Left arm but the specialists were confident he would get movement back. (They were not saying how much). Now it was a waiting game, until the wound had healed sufficiently, for him to return to Emerald, where he would be receiving physiotherapy for some time. When Bev told Gerry that Spider was back in custody, and would be going to trial in three weeks time, Gerry was elated. Tom got home that night after midnight, but Eli was waiting for him, and he had to explain everything that had happened. Tom flew down to see his mate, on day three, and he was surprised at how good he looked. It appeared the wound to his left upper arm was significant, and would require much physio. Gerry sounded very positive, and said he was going to be at the trial. He explained the wound started on the outside of the left upper arm and continued under the arm, and up towards the centre on the inside of the arm. The medical team were amazed, at what they were able to accomplish. This was due in part to the fact that Gerry was very fit.

Down at the police station things were abuzz, Spider was checked on every half hour and this annoyed him intensely. There was nothing he could do, the police were happy. The public prosecutor was very busy, getting the enormous amount of evidence supplied by Danny Bell, into some sort of order. He would discuss with Judge Mason how much of the evidence would actually be needed at trial as there was a mountain of evidence. Some of it would be considered repetitive and surplus to requirements. The public prosecutor would in the time available, prepare his case deciding on how to approach the issues. The order in which to do so, to ensure the facts blended to make a clear picture of how this atrocious deed had been perpetrated. As only one week had been set aside by judge Mason for the case it was obvious that the prosecutor would only use the most telling evidence at trial. The judge had decided the case would be heard on the week starting the 18th of the month. Now that Spider was out of the way Eddie was determined to take over. He thought, he knew, what there was to know, so he put out his directive, comply, but Eddie did not have the, narcissistic attribute to run a drug ring. He would fold, the runners had no desire to work for him as he slacked the ability to project authority, he was no leader.

In the local newspaper, Tom and George were hailed as heroes for their acts of bravery, in thwarting Spider's vile attempt, to murder Gerry Keane. This did not do their businesses any harm. If they had not been well known in Emerald before, they certainly were now. Gerry returned to Emerald with his arm in a sling. He had movement of all four fingers and the thumb, so that was a blessing, but the physiotherapist Beth said Gerry, would need plenty of special exercise for that arm. She believed, he could regain much of his movement, if not all. Gerry went down to the medical centre, every day and Beth gave him exercises to do when not with her. One of the exercises was, squeezing a squash ball repeatedly.

Bev and Jane were much relieved to have Gerry home, and Bev was amazed at his determination, to get his arm right again. Gerry pointed out to Bev the trial would cover Shirley's assassination, so she should think about whether she wanted to hear that. Tom had spoken to Eli saying the trial would be very bad. He could not stop her going, and he would not try to. However she would find it very traumatic, and he was worried for her. Eli said she recognised this fact, but she had to know, and she hoped Tom would be by her side. Eli, Tom, Bev and Gerry all ended up sitting together in a row at the trial.

The trial was due to start on the following Monday, so judge Mason got hold of the public prosecutor and told him. As many people would be wanting to see the trial, it would be held in court one and played over a TV screen in court two, for those who were unable to find seating in court one. The accused who was housed in an internal cell, to prevent any outside interference, would be brought up early, in his handcuffs and leg shackles and then the shackles would be bolted to the floor of the court, through the top of the counter. There were two of the strongest constables responsible for bringing him to court, and returning him to his cell. No one, was to speak to the accused and he was not, to know the name of any of the police dealing with him.

Monday arrived, and before the courts were open to the public, Spider was in the dock, but could not be seen as a white film had been applied to the barrier windows surrounding the dock to prevent, any communication with the accused. Once everybody was present one of the police entrusted with his care, removed the film. The judge made the following statement before the proceedings began. He said, "This was a truthful rendition of the facts, and in it, would be statements, which were not for children's ears. Some adults might find the facts too horrific to contemplate, so when that stage was reached the public would be alerted.". The judge then asked the prosecutor to read the indictments.

- Charge one:- wilfully causing the death of Shirley Edwards on the afternoon of 18th May at or near the fisherman's co op.
- Charge two:- wilfully escaping from lawful custody from Maloney Prison, Emerald.
- Charge three:- attempting to assassinate one, Gerry Keane, with a large dagger outside "George's Pub" on the evening of 12th April.

The defendant pleaded not guilty to all charges. As this trial was by judge only, it simplified many issues. The prosecutor went on to say the court has, but one witness for the prosecution who will be heard but not seen. His detailed evidence will be heard in his voice, as he explains the unfolding saga to his interviewer. He was asked, how he got involved with Spider, and he said, "he was sitting in his car one day when Spider jumped into the passenger seat and said drive. He knew Spider by reputation, having heard he was not to be associated with, as he was pure evil. Now Danny had no wish to be assaulted, and then forced to become, his driver. He complied and drove, this was very upsetting for Danny as he had been trying to contact his friends. So they could return to the big city to their employment. Spider would not let him out of his sight. Initially, it was interesting driving around. Once he heard that Spider was a drug dealer he wanted out, but he was being watched all the time. He was forced to sleep in the same room as Spider. Smoking weed was not the best way to retain control of his operations and his consumption of it seemed to increase his rage, as he became more violent. If one of his runners lost a package or did something stupid Spider, would beat him up and tell him to get lost. He would get another runner, these were good jobs with good money if you applied yourself."

"Spider would tell Danny in the morning, to take him down to "George's Pub" and Spider would get a beer for himself and a coke for Danny. They would hang out down there in the snooker room, until they got a call to action. Then they would leave. The something, usually involved drugs, Danny said "his mum told him long ago to keep away from drugs and liquor and not to tell lies". So that is what he did." The interviewer next asked, Danny about the day Rodney came into the snooker room at "George's Pub" to ask Spider to do something for him. Danny went on, "that morning in the snooker room, Spider pulled out a gun from the back of his pants, and showed him. Danny was scared stiff. Spider went on to say it had a silencer on it. Spider said he had been entrusted with keeping the gun safe, as it was "hot," having been used in a murder in the city. Spider quickly returned it to his pants behind his back, as he heard someone coming."

At this time Judge Mason said the court would adjourn and reconvene at 2 pm. The court resumed hearing the witness say, "I was so upset at seeing the handgun I had to go to the toilet. When I returned Rodney Pleasant was talking to Spider. I heard Spider say that will cost you two hundred. Then Rodney left. Later, after they had a bar lunch they went for a ride around town, as Spider was looking for a white convertible car. He did not elaborate why. Sure enough they saw this car driving down Little Street. So they did a U turn and went after it. The car turned into Brown Street and when they got there they could not see it. So Spider said drive around to the alley, at the back that runs, between the two rows of houses. They parked there and Spider said they should walk down the alley looking through the wooden slats of the fencing and see what they could see. Suddenly they heard a house door close and they looked through the slats and saw a woman getting into a white BMW. Knowing they could not get around to the street in time Spider sat down and smoked a zoll." The judge said now would be an appropriate time to adjourn for the day.

Day 2 Judge Mason warned, that what was coming up was better unheard. The witness continued. "A few days later in the afternoon about 5 p.m., they drove north across the bridge and there they saw the car, the white BMW, on it's way to the fisherman's co-op. Spider instructed me to follow the car down there. When we got close, Spider said park behind her, but to the right a bit." Here the judge stopped the proceedings to warn the public that the next ten minutes of the recording was best not listened to by children and adults who could not tolerate violence. The witness continued, "This I did, we waited for a while and a lovely lady came out of the co-op and walked towards her car. As she was about to get into her car, Spider jumped out and pulled the woman around by her right upper arm. The lady reacted by dispatching a vicious kick with her left foot at Spider's groin. Spider seemed to sway, and staggered back from the impact. The lady made an effort to get into her car. Spider pulled the gun out of his pants at the back, and shot the woman twice." THERE WAS A SHRIEK OF HORROR FROM THE WHOLE COURT. The judge stopped the recording, and asked the people to settle. The recording was off for about five minutes until, the court was quiet again. Many people in the audience were weeping. Then the recording continued. "Spider jumped back into the car and said Go! Go! Go! I drove north along Wharf Street, then left into North Street, and right into the road out of town. Spider was absolutely enraged, that a woman could imagine, that she could take him on. Spider said we had to go to Eden until the heat was off."

"Spider was fuming, the woman only had herself to blame, as she had the temerity to try to resist him. She, was entirely responsible for what happened, for being stupid enough to take him on. He had no time for woman, they were only there for man's pleasure, and to raise children. He told Danny not to exceed the speed limit. All the way back to Eden, Spider was saying it was the woman's fault, that she got shot, and Danny just kept quiet. He was petrified Spider might shoot him too, as he was the only witness, to the dreadful deed. They arrived in Eden and went to the house of a relative of Spider. Here they were given a backroom, with a door to the exterior. This suited them just fine, as they could come and go as they pleased. Danny was finding it very hard to cope with all the murder and mayhem, he was quite depressed, and wanted to get back home. Spider beat up some guys, and got into trouble but he seemed unfazed."

Judge Mason called an adjournment for lunch. After the court reconvened the witness continued. "One afternoon, quite a few months later, Spider said, they should take a drive through Emerald to see how things looked. So they entered Emerald from the north went down over the bridge. They turned into Little Street, left in Brown Street then left again back up to the centre of south Emerald. They crossed the bridge again, and Spider said pull over near the bakery I'll get us a pie. Danny pulled over a few doors further down the road, and Spider got out to go for the pies. All the time Danny was watching him in a wing mirror. Spider approached the bakery, but the old man was not in sight. However there was a very attractive redhead standing at corner of the counter, as if to go into the back.

Spider wasted no time. He walked up to her, put his arm around her and tried to draw her close to him. Natalie let out a cry, and in seconds, Jack was there he pulled Natalie to his left, and planted a huge fist in Spider's face, breaking his nose and loosening three teeth. Spider landed on the concrete out cold. Danny watched the scene play out, in the wing mirror of the car. He immediately appeared on the pavement, rushed over, apologised and half dragged, half carried Spider to the car and they sped off. Spider kept asking Danny who had hit him, and Danny said he did not see. Back in Eden Danny could see Spider needed medical treatment so he took him straight to the hospital. They waited a while and then the doctor said Spider had a broken nose and three loose front teeth. The nose would have to heal over time and he should have the loose teeth removed."

"Later when they returned to Emerald, at Mrs.

Mathews boarding house. Danny just could not take this any more he had to go home. One morning he heard Spider getting up, he just pretended to still be asleep as it was early. Spider thinking Danny would sleep for a while yet, went out to smoke marijuana away from the house. As soon as he left, Danny jumped up and grabbed his meagre belongings got in his car and went south. After Danny realised he was rid of Spider, he felt tremendous relief. He went straight to see his mum and told her some of the horrible things he had seen. His mum said he should try not to think of them. He got his old job again as cleaner for the council and was happy to be home, but these memories troubled Danny." Judge Mason said this was a suitable time to adjourn for the day.

Day 3 The witness continued. "After he had been home for quite some time, a nice man came to see him. He said his name was Gerry. "How is it going "Gerry asked Danny, "much better than in Emerald," Danny replied. "I do not know my way around this area," said Gerry. "Well I am finished now," said Danny. I need to wash up then I will help you." Danny packed his tools away, washed up and returned to Gerry. "I am Danny Bell," he said. Gerry introduced himself saying "he was much obliged for

Danny's help as he was quite lost in this part of the big city." "Don't worry, I am finished now. I will take you to a good restaurant just up the road. Come with me," Danny said. They walked up a couple of streets turned left and in a few minutes they were in a good restaurant. Gerry led Danny to an empty table in the back corner and said "choose whatever you like Danny." The waitress wrote the orders down. Danny wanted a hamburger, fries and a coke. Gerry opted for a cappuccino and a ham and tomato sandwich. So they talked about this and that until the food arrived. Danny wasted no time getting stuck into the hamburger. Gerry said, "did you hear Spider is inside for four years" and Danny's replied, "wish they would get him for shooting that lovely lady that did nothing wrong". Gerry very nearly choked. "Yes that was very bad,"said Gerry. Danny replied "I was sitting in the car watching, but I did not know what he was up to. I was petrified he would shoot me too," Danny said. Gerry thought WOW -what have we here ! After finishing their meal Gerry, said "it was very bad what Spider did. Would Danny like to help the authorities lock him up for that". "Yes he would like that." Danny said."I'll tell you what, Gerry said, we'll tell your boss you need to accompany me on official business to see justice done, then we'll go to

your digs to get you things, but you will be back."
Danny said "that was good."

"Everything I have said is the truth as I know it, I am just very upset it had to happen" Danny said. Judge Mason asked the accused if had anything to say, and he replied it was all lies. Count 2 of the indictment The prison warder and the police gave accounts of Spider escaping from Maloney's Prison. However they were unable to explain how this was effected. Count 3 of the indictment now came before Judge Mason. Tom and George were called as witnesses to recount the incident outside the courtyard of George's Hotel on the evening of the 8th. Tom told how he saw Spider make a desperate plunge towards Gerry with a dagger in his right hand. Acting on instinct Tom pushed Gerry hoping to get him out of harms way but unfortunately Spider, with out stretched arm, was able to inflict a serious wound to Gerry's left upper arm which bled profusely. George's evidence was the same as Tom's except for the fact that he had forced Spider to the ground and sat on his back. Judge Mason adjourned the court and said "they would reconvene at 10 am. in one week's time for sentencing." Both Tom and Gerry had to deal with very traumatised wives. However this would, in some way, be ameliorated by the sentence judge Mason was about to give the following week.

As the court convened on the day of sentencing, Judge Mason waited till the court was quiet and started. "What we have heard and experienced over the past weeks is the atrocious behaviour of someone who behaves, as if he has no soul. He has descended to a stage of depravity, which is difficult for the average person to contemplate or comprehend. He is completely devoid of feeling. He considers his wants and desires to the exclusion of all others. It is as if he is the only one on this earth. He is a complete narcissist, who is determined to get his way at any cost, to others. Therefore it is incumbent on this court, to protect society from this deviant in accordance with the way the laws of our land have been written." Spider was told to stand for sentencing.

"Judge Mason began, Spider Kelly I hereby sentence you as follows:

- **On count 1, to 30 years,**
- **On count 2, I sentence you to an additional 2 years on top of your original 4 year term,**
- **On count 3, you are sentenced to a period of 5 years,**

- **All sentences to run consecutively.**

Take him down."

The Edwards and the Keane families felt no elation, they just felt a sense of some justice. They would still have to live, with their loss. However they would at least know what happened, even if it did not make any sense. Tom and Eli were very grateful to Gerry, for his part in seeing that justice was done. On doctors advice Don Williams was not allowed to be at the trial, but Tom kept him informed about the result. Don was grateful that they finally knew what had transpired, but it left him numb. This was the end of an horrific chapter in the lives of the families of Emerald. Now they needed to heal and move forward. Gerry was not one to give up, so after the court case he started going back to the office each day for the morning, after physio at 8am.His staff gave him a big cheer, on his return to work. Gerry did as much as he could, at work each day, which was substantial by normal standards. Initially he found that he could only manage a morning, so he left enough work for the secretaries to keep them busy all day. He continued his physio with Beth, and although it hurt like hell, he was not giving up. He was not prepared to let Spider, have any influence over his life.

It is a sad fact of life, that there are always those who are determined to take advantage of others. Usually the weaker members of society, to cause mayhem and destruction, by plying them with drugs and other mind blowing stimulants. As these drugs are addictive, the peddler is certain of a market for his dreadful supplies. Not just a market but a growing number of individuals who are enticed, to try these mind disturbing substances. Through this whole process of destroying others lives there is absolutely no sense of guilt, shame, or pity, on the part of the narcissist. He believes he has a right to exploit anyone he comes across, as they are not obliged to purchase his wares, but ask for them. The fact that these substances are illegal, for a very good reason, is of no consequence to the trader, he is only concerned in their sale. There is a complete absence, of any understanding of the fact that we are all on this planet and the best way forward is to pull together, not try to destroy each other.

THIRTY-THREE

After the trial Danny was keen to see Gerry. He was distressed to see what Spider had done to him. He felt partly responsible for causing this injury to Gerry. However Gerry assured him it was over now, and he need not be concerned. Gerry told Danny he had done a wonderful job of telling the truth to the court. He offered to get Danny back to his mum in the southern suburbs. He pointed out that he was unable to drive. So his good friend Tom would drive and he would go along. Danny was happy with this suggestion. Between Tom and Gerry they would organise it. Gerry spoke to Sgt. Fred Lewis and pointed out Danny needed to be returned to his mum without anybody knowing about it. Gerry said all the drug pushers knew his BMW so they would have to use another car.

It was around this time that the nursing aid looking after Mrs. Stokes arrived one day to find

Mrs. Stokes unresponsive in her wheelchair. She immediately phoned for ambulance support, and the medics were there in a matter of minutes. They examined Mrs. Stokes and said she had a very weak pulse, so they rushed her to emergency at the hospital in Eden. Natalie and Jack were told of Mrs. Stokes serious condition, and Gerry told Natalie to go to her mother. Jack asked Olaf if he minded looking after the bakery for a while, and he said he would be happy to. So Jack took Natalie to Eden Hospital to see how her mother was. The doctors said her condition was very serious, and they would know more in the next few hours.

Natalie and Jack were allowed into her the ward, where Mrs. Stokes was the only patient. She was receiving oxygen, and there was a drip attached to her hand. She was attached to a machine monitoring her vital signs. Natalie sat near her mum holding her hand and speaking to her, but there was no response. The situation remained serious, and the nursing staff attended to her regularly. Natalie and Jack remained with Mrs. Stokes until she passed away peacefully that evening, without regaining consciousness. Natalie was devastated, she had lived for her mother until Jack came along. Now fortunately she still had Jack, who was always there to provide support. Four days later Mrs. Stokes was cremated as she had requested. Natalie gradually managed to get over her mother's passing, and Jack had played an important role, in getting Natalie to accept that her mum was in a better place now.

After some weeks, Jack started rearranging the furniture in the house, to suite their requirements, as Natalie and he were alone in the house, now. It was right that they feel comfortable in their home. Natalie was very grateful to Jack as the way the setup was, kept reminding her of her mum, and making her depressed. A plumber was brought in to make some alterations to the plumbing in the room Mrs. Stokes had occupied. After Jack had done some painting things were much improved. So what they now had was a three bedroom house with lounge, dining room, kitchen, bathroom, toilet and back and front verandahs. Natalie was very dependent on Jack, and he wondered if something could be done to take her mind off the tragic loss of her mother. It was the time after work each day that she really seemed to suffer most. Natalie needed something else, to occupy her mind.

It was decided, an attempted break in at one of the factories would be instigated. Tom would respond as well as two police cars, one police car with Danny lying on the floor at the back. At the factory concerned the vehicles would go inside the factory and Danny would be transferred to Tom's car. After the police cars had left, Tom would go around to Gerry's offices and park at the back as usual, and Danny would move to the car, of Gerry's partner, Mitchell Field. Tom with dark spectacles, and a cap, and Gerry slumped in the passenger seat would deliver Danny, back to his home in the southern suburbs. Gerry told Danny, he was a hero for what he had done. He suggested Danny stay down in the suburbs that he knew, as it was safer for him. Danny said he would and he shook hands with them and Gerry and Tom left.

Gerry continued his physio and slowly his Left arm improved. However after a year it was apparent he had just over 90% use of the arm. It was not possible for Gerry to straighten his left arm completely. and it lacked certain twisting motion, but Gerry was okay with that. He felt it was a price he was prepared to pay, to bring justice for his friends, Tom, Eli and of course for Bev his wife and himself. When he walked normally, his left arm movement looked unnatural. The only ones noticing this, were those closely involved in the events. These terrible events, had ensured that Tom and Gerry became as close as twins, and they would communicate on a daily basis. Gerry was as much a hero of this tragedy, as Tom and George, going out of his way to track down Danny Bell, and bringing him back to Emerald to give his evidence. Without Gerry there would have been no closure.

Chap asked George if he could visit again, and George agreed. They met one evening in the usual place and exchanged pleasantries. Chap said it was quite a while since they met, and much had happened. George told Chap about the attempted murder of Gerry, and how he and Tom had managed to foil the attacker, Spider. Chap was astounded, and inquired as to Gerry's condition. George said Gerry had suffered a bad wound, to his upper left arm. If the surgeons had not operated as soon as they did, then Gerry could have been left with an arm that could not function. So everybody was relieved to see how well, Gerry survived the dreadful attack. He was obliged to undergo painful physiotherapy for the best part of a year, but he never complained.

As far as the family were concerned things were progressing very well. The bakery was paid up, and there was no debt. Chap asked if he had found out anything about the building the bakery was in. George said he had. He had spoken to Olaf, who knew the owners, and they might just be willing to entertain an offer. However they would not say how much they might be expecting for the building. Chap said I see. Chap said we will talk again on this issue. He then finished his Johnny Walker black label and said good night. George sat there silently with a puzzled look on his face. He had much to think about.

George made an appointment to see Gerry and arrived at the appointed time. He enquired as to how well Gerry was feeling, and if the wound interfered with his performing his activities. Gerry said he was making good progress, but some movements were quite exhausting. George said to Gerry that Jack and Natalie were living in the house, which Natalie had inherited on the death of Mrs. Stokes. Peter was now alone, in the house that George owned. He felt maybe they should be looking at a better use of their finances. The building that housed the bakery, was a double storey, with a shop next to the bakery, and two, two bedroom flats above. The shop next to the bakery was occupied by a news agency, that had been there for some years. If that building could be purchased at a reasonable price maybe they could sell their house, and buy the building and Peter could stay in one of the flats above the shop. Gerry asked George if he had any idea of the value of his house, George said he had an evaluation of $295,000.

Furthermore he had asked Olaf who knew the owners of the building to see if they might sell. They were talking in the region of $350,000. So Gerry said, let us get permission for a pre- purchase inspection of the building from the owners. The owners agreed believing they might make a killing. Gerry asked an inspector he knew, for a thorough inspection of the building. This was performed, and it came back with some questions with regard to the brickwork in the dividing wall, between the bakery and the shop and flats. It would not be passed by the inspector in the condition it was in at present. This information was conveyed to the owners, who began doing some back pedalling. Asking if they lowered the price, and the buyer accepted the responsibility of having the work done would that satisfy the authorities.

The prospective buyers said how much would they lower the asking price, as the work would be quite expensive. The owners asked the buyer to make an offer. So Gerry on George's behalf said $310,000, and they would have the wall fixed. After a few days the owner came back, agreeing to the terms. Gerry asked Chap again if he could help with a loan and he said he would. A month later Jack became the proud owner of the building housing the bakery and news agency, with two flat upstairs. A local bricklayer carried out some repairs to the wall between the bakery and the Shop and it passed inspection. Having the newsagent next to the bakery was a winner, as it encouraged the public visiting one outlet to visit the other as well.

Peter was very pleased having his own flat just a short distance from the hotel and bar. He did not desire female company, as he was quite happy on his own. His idea of the opposite sex, was not very glowing. He found them, to have agendas, and they were not straight talkers. He was not one for drama and disliked someone lying to him. He was a straight forward guy with no hidden schemes. He could not tolerate intrigue. Peter believed he would end up, part owner of the hotel and pub along with his sister Michelle, and he was okay with that as they got along just fine. As a person, Peter enjoyed listening to music, as he found it very soothing and relaxing. After a day in the pub serving customers, he enjoyed a little peace. He would put on a C.D. and relax in his favourite chair, listening to the music and watching the fish in his big fish tank.

THIRTY-FOUR

Gary and Shirley were developing very well, Gary had red hair and hazel eyes. Shirley was a brunette with beautiful blue eyes like her mother. Eli, in spite of all the trauma, felt very blessed she had Tom and two wonderful children. This did a lot to help ease the pain, that she felt at losing her best friend. Tom and Eli brought their children up to appreciate nature. The children loved Eli's dog, Honey and spent much time playing with her. Honey would follow them around as if she was their guardian angel. Gary would join the "nippers" in the lifesavers programme as soon as he was old enough to. Tom was very happy, that his son and daughter loved the water as much as he did.

Tom continued to spend as much time as he could with his family, without neglecting his businesses. He had tremendous fun playing with Shirley and Gary on the lawn outside, teaching them different exercises. They all swam as often as they could, and Tom and Eli were happy with their development. One of the games they played was trying to tread water and throwing the ball to each other. This really helped the two young ones learn how to tread water. Both Tom, and Eli discussed things with their children to create a bonding, showing them that issues that arise, are talked about at home. Nothing was off the table, when they felt they needed to say something, or ask a question. That was how people learned in life. Gary was now 4 and Shirley nearly two, their little bodies showed that they had experienced good exercise as the little muscles were forming in their arms and legs.

Gerry and Bev had Jane's, success at school, and her wonderful progress in her music. She was doing very well at high school and this helped to deaden the grief they still felt at Shirley's assassination. Bev slowly recovered, from the trauma of the court case, and continued her work at the boutique, she and Eli spoke to each other, every day. Gerry was perhaps the one that paid the highest price. He had lost a good friend in Shirley, and he had nearly lost his left arm. However Gerry saw it differently to the others. He had managed with his dogged determination, to track down the sole witness, that could put Spider

Kelly away for a long time, and he did it for his friends Tom and Eli and of course for Bev. This along with his deep friendship with Tom was all the satisfaction he needed. The one downside was he was unable to play squash, as the left arm caused him to lose his balance when moving at speed. Apart from that he had learned, about a young fellow, named Danny, who saw life differently to the average person. He believed in always telling the truth, being committed to his job, and staying away from drugs and alcohol, because his mother had told him so. He might have lacked ambition but his other attributes, made him worth his weight in gold.

Tom would progress. He had lost Shirley, but he now had Eli who he loved deeply, and two wonderful children, whom he would do his utmost to help develop to their full potential. Gerry had become a wonderful friend to him and his family and he was very grateful for this. Eli in spite of all the trauma, felt very blessed, she had Tom and two beautiful children, she was happy. Slowly the families affected by this terrible tragedy began to put their lives together again. If Eli had not had Tom, and the little ones she would have been in a very bad place. These three in her life, lifted her up so she could see, that good things, can come from disaster.

Helen Pleasant and her two girls bore the brunt of these horrific events. It was very painful to face the town, knowing her husband, and their father was responsible for setting this egregious chain of events in motion. After a while Helen and her mother and Helens two girls sold the house, changed their names and moved to a town up the coast where they were unknown.

The programme with wayward boys, was continued, by Gerry with very good results overall. The police could not understand how he could carry on, without becoming depressed. Gerry saw every young boy, as a new challenge, with his own set of problems. His task was, to release the youth from his perceived restraints, and allow him to see life, as a wonderful opportunity. This was probably due to the fact, that he enjoyed trying to understand, how each youth sees life. Each boy seemed to have a particular way of looking, at what their future would hold, not allowing for the fact that nothing happens the way you think it will.

Gerry went on to write a programme that he followed, when dealing with the wayward boys. It detailed, all the factors that he had found, to be useful in his approach. Some ideas worked, in some cases and others worked in some, or all cases. The most important issue Gerry could identify was, the way in which the boys, were initially addressed and accepted. The approach being the first contact, was of paramount importance, as it set the tone for all further engagement. In subsequent meetings it was possible to build on that very first impression, the youth got from the guide. This helped to re-enforce the fact, that the guide had no feeling of superiority, animosity or aversion towards the individual. Just a hope, for agreement, on some fundamental issues. The sessions were as long as the youth felt comfortable with. He was encouraged to continue his association with the surf life savers, down at the beach, as agreed to, at the first meeting. What Gerry could not impart to others was his gentle, unassuming and almost disinterested manner of engagement, that was unique to his approach. This was the mesmerising way of a truly gifted person, offering a hand of friendship without any expectation of an affirmative response.